"Why the hell has your witchy face been in my head for the past fifteen years?"

McVey didn't expect an answer. He wasn't even sure why he'd asked the question. True, she looked very much like the woman in his recurring dream, but the longer he stared at her—couldn't help that part, unfortunately—the more the differences added up.

On closer inspection, Amara's hair really was more brown than red. Her features were also significantly finer than...whoever. Her gray eyes verged on charcoal, her slim curves were much better toned and her legs were the longest he'd seen on any woman anywhere.

He might have lingered on the last thing if she hadn't slapped a hand to his chest, narrowed those beautiful eyes to slits and seared him with a glare.

"What the hell kind of question is that?"

NIGHT OF THE RAVEN

JENNA RYAN

HARLEQUIN® INTRIGUE®

To Anne Stuart, who got the writing ball rolling for me.
Thank you, Anne, for all the great books.

Recycling programs
for this product may
not exist in your area.

ISBN-13: 978-0-373-69799-1

Night of the Raven

Copyright © 2014 by Jacqueline Goff

HARLEQUIN®
www.Harlequin.com

Printed in U.S.A.

ABOUT THE AUTHOR

Jenna started making up stories before she could read or write. As she grew up, romance always had a strong appeal, but romantic suspense was the perfect fit. She tried out a number of different careers, including modeling, interior design and travel, but writing has always been her one true love. That and her longtime partner, Rod.

Inspired from book to book by her sister Kathy, she lives in a rural setting fifteen minutes from the city of Victoria, British Columbia. It's taken a lot of years, but she's finally slowed the frantic pace and adopted a West Coast mindset. Stay active, stay healthy, keep it simple. Enjoy the ride, enjoy the read. All of that works for her, but what she continues to enjoy most is writing stories she loves. She also loves reader feedback. Email her at jacquigoff@shaw.ca or visit Jenna Ryan on Facebook.

Books by Jenna Ryan

HARLEQUIN INTRIGUE

CAST OF CHARACTERS

Amara Bellam—She returned to Raven's Hollow, her ancestral home, seeking refuge from a vindictive crime lord.

Ethan McVey—A man of many secrets, the new Raven's Cove police chief will do all he can to protect Amara.

Jake Blume—Amara's witchy ancestors have always frightened the Raven's Cove deputy.

Lazarus Blume—Amara's straight-laced uncle has money—and a great deal to hide.

Yolanda Bellam—She runs the Red Eye bar in Raven's Hollow, and she doesn't like her job, or Amara.

Brigham Blume—There's no love lost between the burly raven tamer and anyone bearing the name Bellam.

RJ Blume—He has cared for his aging uncle Lazarus for many years.

Hannah Blume—Her death is a mystery. But was it brought about by a crime lord or someone with a personal grudge?

Westor Hall—He knows all about McVey's secret past.

Willy Sparks—The crime lord who wants Amara dead has sent a member of his extended family to do the job for him.

Chapter One

Los Angeles, California
15 years ago

The scene felt so real, McVey figured this time it might not be unfolding in his head. His totally messed-up head, which wasn't improving thanks to the dream that had haunted him every night for the past two weeks.

The moment he fell asleep, he found himself trapped in an attic room that smelled like old wood, wet dirt and something far more pungent than boiled cabbage. The air was muggy and strangely alive. Thunder crashed every few seconds and tongues of lightning flickered through a curtain of fetid gray smoke.

He knew he was hiding, hunkered down in some shadowy corner where the two people he watched—barely visible within the smoke—couldn't see him.

The man's fingers clenched and unclenched. The woman circled a small fire and muttered unintelligible words.

Two violent thunderbolts later, only the woman and the smoke remained. The man had vanished.

Okay, that couldn't be good. McVey searched frantically for a way out of wherever he was before whoever *she* was saw him and made him eat the same black dripping thing she'd given the now-gone man.

With her eyes closed and her hair and clothes askew, she mumbled and swayed and breathed in choking fumes. Then suddenly she froze. In the next flash of lightning her head began to turn. Slowly, creepily, like a rusty weather vane in a bad horror film.

Her eyes locked on McVey's hiding place. He heard the black thing in her hand plop to the floor. She raised a dripping finger and pointed it straight at him.

"You," she accused in a voice that made him think of rusty nails soaked in whiskey. "You saw what passed between me and the one she would have you call Father."

Whoa, McVey thought on an unnatural spurt of fear. That was a whole lot, what she'd just said. A whole lot of nothing he understood, or wanted to.

"You have no business here, child." She started toward him. "Don't you know I'm mad?"

Right. Mad. So why the hell couldn't he move his—? He stopped the question abruptly, backpedaled and latched on to the other word. Child?

Shock, slick and icy, rolled through him when he looked down and saw his feet encased in tiny, shin-high boots.

Thunder rattled the house. His head shot up when he heard a low creak. Watching her smile, he realized with a horrified jolt that she was beautiful. He also realized he knew her, or at least he recognized her.

When she pointed at him again, the spell broke and he reached for his gun on the nightstand. Except there was no nightstand, and the next streak of lightning revealed a hand that wasn't his. Couldn't be. It was too small, too pale and far too delicate.

"Don't be afraid, child." Her voice became a silky croon. Her ugly clothes and hair melted into a watery blur of color. "I won't harm you. I'll only make what you think you've seen go away."

McVey wanted to tell her that he had no idea what he'd seen and the only thought in his head right then was to get out of there before her finger—still dripping with something disgusting—touched him.

He edged sideways in the dark. He could escape if the lightning would give him a break.

Of course it didn't, and her eyes, gray and familiar, continued to track his every move.

"There's no way out," she warned. With an impatient sound she grabbed his wrists. "I don't want to hurt you. You know I never have."

No, he really didn't know that, but wherever he was, he had no gun. Or strength, apparently, to free himself from her grasp.

She laughed when he fought her. "Foolish child. You forget I'm older than you. I'm also more powerful, and much, much meaner than your mother."

His mother?

She dragged him out of the corner. "Come with me."

When she hauled him upright, he stumbled. Looking down, he saw the hem of the long dress he'd stepped on.

"Why am I…?" But when he heard the high, unfamiliar voice that emerged from his throat, he choked the question off.

The woman crouched to offer a grim little smile. "Believe me when I tell you, Annalee, what I will do to you this night is for your own good…."

McVey SHOT FROM the nightmare on the next peal of thunder. The dark hair that fell over his eyes made him think he'd gone blind. A gust of wind rattled the shade above his nightstand and he spotted the stuttering neon sign outside. It wasn't until he saw his own hand reaching over to check his gun that he let himself fall back onto the mattress and worked on loosening the knots in his stomach.

That they remained there, slippery yet stubbornly tight, was only partly due to the recurring nightmare. The larger part stemmed from a more tangible source.

It was time to do what he'd known he would do for the past two weeks, ever since his nineteenth birthday. Ever since his old man had pried a deathbed promise from his only son.

He would set aside the disturbing fact that every time he fell asleep these days he turned into a young girl who wore long dresses and old-fashioned boots. He'd forget about the woman he thought he should know who wanted to give him amnesia. He'd focus strictly on keeping the promise he'd made to his father. If that meant turning his back on the people he'd worked with since…well, not all that long actually, so nothing lost there. He was going to walk away now, tonight, keep his promise and change the course of his life.

Maybe if he did that, the nightmare would stay where it belonged. Buried deep in the past of the person he feared he'd once been.

Chapter Two

New Orleans, Louisiana
Present Day

"Make no mistake about it…"

Moments after the sentence had been passed, the raspy-voiced man with the stooped shoulders and the tic in his left eye had looked straight at Amara Bellam and whispered just loud enough for her and the two men beside her to hear.

"Those who brought about my imprisonment will pay. My family will see to it."

Although her eyewitness testimony had played a large part in his conviction, at the time Jimmy Sparks had uttered his threat, Amara had thought his reaction was nothing more than knee-jerk. After all, life in prison for someone of his dubious health surely meant he wouldn't see the free light of day ever again.

But the word *family* crept into her head more and more often as the weeks following his incarceration crept by. It took root when Lieutenant Michaels of the New Orleans Police Department contacted her with the news that one of her two fellow witnesses, Harry Benedict, was dead.

"Now, don't panic." Michaels patted the air in front of her. "Remember, Harry had close to two decades on Jimmy."

"Lieutenant, Jimmy Sparks is the two-pack-a-day head of a large criminal family. He has a dozen relatives to do his legwork. Harry was a hale and hearty seventy-nine-year-old athlete who hiked across Maryland just last year."

"Which is very likely why he died of a massive coronary just last night." The detective made another useless patting motion. "Really, you don't need to panic over this."

"I'm not panicking."

"No, you're not." His hand dropped. "Well, that makes one of you. Chad, our overstressed third witness, knocked back two glasses of bourbon while I was explaining the situation."

"Chad dived off the temperance wagon right after Jimmy Sparks whispered his threat to us." She rubbed her arms. "Are you sure Harry died of natural causes?"

"The path lab said it was heart failure, pure and simple. The man had a history, Amara. Two significant attacks in the past five years."

Hale and hearty, though, she recalled after Michaels left.

For the next few weeks she fought her jitters with an overload of work. Even so, fear continued to curl in Amara's stomach. She had thought she might be starting to get past it when the harried lieutenant appeared on her doorstep once again.

"Chad's dead." She saw it in his dog-tired expression. "Damn."

The lieutenant spread his fingers. "I'm sorry, Amara. And before you ask, the official cause, as determined by the coroner's office, is accidental suicide."

"This is not happening." A shiver of pure terror snaked through her system. When the detective spoke her name, she raised both hands. "Please don't try to convince me that suicides can't be arranged."

"Of course they can, but Chad Weaver was surrounded by eleven friends when he collapsed—in his home, at a party arranged by him and to which he invited every person in attendance. No one crashed the event, and the drugs and alcohol he ingested were his own."

She swung around to stare. "Chad took drugs?"

"Like the booze, he got into them after Jimmy Sparks's trial. As witnesses, you all had—er, have—impeccable credentials."

"Right. Credentials." Feeling her world had tilted radically, Amara headed for her Garden District balcony and some much needed night air. "Mind's really spinning here, Lieutenant. What kinds of drugs did Chad take?"

The cop rubbed his brow. "Ecstasy, mostly. A little coke. Might've smoked some weed earlier in the day."

She made a negating motion. "No chance that any of those substances could've been tampered with prepurchase, huh?"

"Amara…"

Her sarcastic tone didn't quite mask the anger beginning to churn inside her. "It's a fair question, Lieutenant. We're talking about street dealers, people who aren't exactly pillars of the community. Are you saying that, given the right inducement, not one of them could or would have slipped a little extra something into the goody bags Chad bought?"

"The coroner is convinced it was—"

"Yes, I heard that part. Accidental death."

"Suicide."

It cost her a great deal to work up a smile. "I guess we'll find out, won't we?" She struggled to maintain her composure. "I can read your face, Michaels. You're going to tell me there's nothing you can do in terms of police protection. I mean, on the off chance the coroner is mistaken."

The detective regarded the toes of his scuffed shoes.

"Massive coronary for Harry. Private party for Chad. No one except the three of you and me heard Jimmy's threat. The media would love to jump all over this, but they won't, because the powers that be are well aware of Jimmy Sparks's many and varied connections. Sure, the odd question is bound to surface, but they'll die as quickly as they're born. After all, there's no evidence of wrongdoing in either case."

"I suppose not. Well, then." Amara took a deep breath. "At the risk of sounding paranoid, do you have any suggestions as to how I can avoid a date with the forensic team?"

When he raised his head, the steely look in his eyes said it all. "You need to disappear," he told her. "Get out of the city and go someplace safe."

"Safe. Great." She pressed firm fingers into her temples. "Where?"

Tossing a worried look onto the street below, Michaels pulled her away from the wrought iron railing. "Your parents are in South America, aren't they?"

"Central America. They're doing medical relief work, have been for the past two years. Mostly with children, Lieutenant. I'm not taking this nightmare to them."

"You have relatives in Maine, don't you?"

"What? Yes—no."

"We'll go with the first answer." When the lights bobbed, he closed the French doors and pulled the curtains. "Let's do it this way. You pack, make whatever calls you need to, and I'll drive you to the airport." He managed a feeble grin. "If there's one thing I'm good at, it's shaking criminal tails."

Amara's mind swam. "Surely Jimmy Sparks's family will have the airport covered."

"Not in Jackson, Mississippi. I know this guy, Amara. It won't be a group hunt so much as a single-person stalk."

"As in one person sent to make sure I choke to death on a bite of crawfish or drop dead on the sidewalk from a nonexistent blood clot that'll dissolve before... God, what am I saying? No, wait, what am I doing?" She turned to face him. "I can't endanger the lives of my family members. You know I can't."

"You can, and you should. Most of those family members live in a spooky little town in a remote and densely wooded section of coastal Maine. Raven's Cove is your best and safest option right now."

She stared at him for five long seconds before countering with a flat "It's Raven's Hollow, and I will call my grandmother. I'll explain the situation. But if she's the least bit hesitant, I'm choosing another destination."

"Deal." He ran his gaze over the ceiling when the lights bobbed again. "Pack only what you need."

What she needed, Amara reflected, was a time machine. Unfortunately all she had was her iPhone, her grandmother's number and a waning glimmer of hope that she'd ever see anyone in or out of Raven's Hollow, Maine, again.

Chapter Three

"I've already broken up two bar fights tonight, Chief, and the crowd here's spoiling for more." Jake Blume's tone, surly at the best of times, soured. "It's gonna be a free-for-all by the time this two-town party—which ain't no kind of party, in my opinion—plays out. Still three days to go and the hooligans on both sides are making their feelings known with their fists." His voice dropped to a growl. "What do you want me to do about tonight's ruckus?"

McVey heard about half of what his griping deputy related. More important to him than a minor barroom scuffle was the TV across the room where the Chicago Cubs were cheerfully mopping up Wrigley Field with his beloved Dodgers.

"Run," he told the slow-motion hitter who'd just slugged the ball to the fence.

"From a bar fight?" Jake gave a contemptuous snort. "This town ain't turned me into a girl yet, McVey."

"Talking to the television, Deputy." Disgusted by yet another out, McVey took a long drink of beer and muted the sound. "Okay, which bar and what kind of damage are we talking about?"

"It's the Red Eye in the Hollow—a town I'm still trying to understand why we're working our butts off to cover so its police chief can sun his sorry ass in Florida for the next couple weeks."

"Man's on his honeymoon, Jake." Amusement glimmered. "The novelty'll wear off soon enough."

His deputy gave another snort. "Said one confirmed bachelor to another."

"I was never confirmed—and that was a ball," he told the onscreen umpire.

"Look, if I'm interrupting…"

"You're not." McVey dangled the beer bottle between his knees and rubbed a tired eye. "I assume the damage at the Red Eye is minimal."

"As bar fights go in these parts."

"Then give whoever threw the first punch a warning, make the participants pay up and remind everyone involved that it's you who's on duty tonight, not me."

"Meaning?"

"You've got a shorter fuse, zero tolerance and, between the towns, six empty jail cells just begging to be filled."

"Good point." Jake cheered up instantly. "Can I threaten to cuff 'em?"

"Your discretion, Deputy. After you're done, head back to the Cove. I'll be in at first light to relieve you."

When he glanced over and saw his team had eked out two hits, McVey gave his head a long, slow roll and sat back to think.

In the fourteen months since he'd arrived in Raven's Cove, he'd only had the dream five times, which was a hell and gone better average than he'd had during his six years with the Chicago Police Department or the nearly eight he'd put in in New York. At least once a month in both places, he'd found himself up in a smoke-filled attic while a woman he still couldn't place told him she was going to screw up his memories. Not that he'd given up city life over anything as nebulous as a dream. His reasons had run a whole lot deeper…. And was that a floorboard he'd just heard creak upstairs?

With the bottle poised halfway to his mouth, he listened, heard nothing and, taking another long swallow, switched his attention back to the TV.

A third run by the Dodgers gave him hope. A screech of hinges from an interior door had him raising his eyes to the ceiling yet again.

Okay, so not alone. And wasn't that a timely thing, considering he'd received two emails lately warning him that a man with secrets should watch the shadows around him very, very closely?

Standing, he shoved his gun into the waistband of his jeans, killed the light and started up the rear stairs.

The wind that had been blowing at near-gale force all day howled around the single-paned windows. Even so, he caught a second creak. He decided his intruder could use a little stealth training. Then he stepped on a sagging tread, heard the loud protest and swore.

The intruder must have heard it, too. The upstairs door that had been squeaking open immediately stopped moving.

Drawing his weapon, McVey gave his eyes another moment to adjust and finished the climb. He placed the intruder in the kitchen. Meaning the guy had the option of slinking out the way he'd entered—through the back door—or holding position to see what developed. Whatever the case, McVey had the advantage in that he'd been living in the house for more than two weeks and had committed the odd layout to memory.

Another door gave a short creak and he pictured the intruder circling.

The anticipation that kindled felt good. Sleepy coastal

towns worked for him on several levels these days. Unfortunately, as action went, they tended to be…well, frankly, dead. Unless you counted the increasing number of bar fights and the sniping of two local factions, each of which had its own legend, and neither of which was willing to admit that both legends had probably been created by an ancient—and presumably bored—Edgar Allan Poe wannabe.

Another blast of wind rattled the panes and sent a damp breeze over McVey's face. It surprised him to see a light burning in the mudroom. Apparently his intruder was extremely stupid, poorly equipped or unaware that he'd broken into the police chief's current residence. The last idea appealed most, but as it also seemed the least likely, McVey continued to ease through the house.

He spotted the shadow just as the wind—he assumed wind—slammed the kitchen door shut. The bang echoed beneath a wicked gust that buffeted the east wall and caused the rafters to moan.

Shoving the gun into his jeans, he went for a low tackle. If the person hadn't swung around and allowed a weak beam of light to trickle through from the mudroom, he would have taken them both hard to the floor. But his brain clicked in just fast enough that he was able to alter his trajectory, snag the intruder by the waist and twist them both around so only he landed on the pine planking.

His head struck the table, his shoulder the edge of a very solid chair. To make matters worse, his trapped quarry rammed an elbow into his ribs, wriggled around and clawed his left cheek.

He caught the raised hand before it could do any serious damage and, using his body weight, reversed their positions. "Knock it—" was all he got out before his instincts kicked in and he blocked the knee that was heading for his groin.

Jesus, enough!

Teeth gnashed and with pain shooting through his skull, he brought his eyes into focus on the stunning and furious face of the woman from his nightmare.

FEAR STREAKED THROUGH Amara's mind, not for her own safety, but for that of her grandmother who'd lived in this house for close to seventy years.

Although she was currently pinned to the floor with her hands over her head and her wrists tightly cuffed, she attempted to knee him again. When that failed, she bucked her hips up into his. If she could loosen his iron grip, she might be able to sink her teeth into his forearm.

"I'll kill you if you've hurt her," she panted. "This is about me, not my family. You of all people should understand that."

He offset another blow. "Lady, the only thing I understand is that you broke into a house that doesn't belong to you."

"Or you," she fired back. "You have no right to be here. Where's my grandmother?"

"I have every right to be here, and how the hell should I know?"

Her heart tripped. "Is she—dead?"

"What? No. Look, I live here, okay?"

Unable to move, Amara glared at him. "You're lying. I spoke to Nana last night. There was no mention of a man either visiting or living in her home."

He lowered his head just far enough for her to see the smile that grazed his lips. "Maybe your granny doesn't tell you everything, angel."

"That's disgusting." She refused to tremble. "Have you hurt her?"

"I haven't done anything to her. I don't eat elderly women, then take to their beds in order to get the jump on their beautiful granddaughters."

"That's not exactly reassuring."

"Yeah, it really is, Red."

When her eyes flashed, he sighed. "Red… Red Riding Hood. Now, why don't you calm down, we'll back up a few steps and try to sort this out? My name's Ethan McVey and I—"

"Have no business being in my grandmother's house."

"You're gonna have to get past that one, I'm afraid. Truth is I have all kinds of business here." He shifted position when she almost liberated her other knee. "As far as I know, your grandmother's somewhere in the Caribbean with two of her friends and one very old man who's sliding down the slippery slope toward his hundred and second birthday."

His words startled a disbelieving laugh out of her. "Nana took old Rooney Blume to the Caribbean?"

"That's the story I got. No idea if it's true. Her private life's not my concern. You, on the other hand, are very much my concern, seeing as you're lying on my kitchen floor behaving like a wildcat."

"Nana's kitchen floor."

"Rent's paid, floor's mine. So's the badge you probably failed to notice on the table above us."

Doubt crept in. "Badge, as in cop?"

"Badge as in chief of police. Raven's Cove," he added before she could ask.

The red haze clouding Amara's vision began to dissolve. "You said *rent*. If you're a cop, why are you renting my grandmother's house?"

"Because the first place she rented to me developed serious plumbing and electrical issues, both of which are in the process of being rectified."

Why a laugh should tickle her throat was beyond her. "Would that first place be Black Rock Cottage, rebuilt from a ruin fifty years ago by my grandfather and renovated last year by Wrecking Ball Buck Blume?"

"That'd be it."

"Then I'm sorry I scratched you."

"Does that mean you're done trying to turn me into a eunuch?"

"Maybe."

"As reassurances go, I'm not feeling it, Red."

"Put yourself in my position. My grandmother didn't mention a Caribbean vacation when I spoke to her yesterday."

"So, thinking she was here, you opted to break and enter your grandmother's home rather than knock on the door."

"I knocked. No one answered. Nana keeps an extra key taped to a flowerpot on her back stoop. And before you tell me how careless that is, mine's bigger."

To her relief, he let go of her wrists and pushed himself to his knees. He was still straddling her, but at least his far too appealing face wasn't quite so close. "Your what?"

"Omission. Nana didn't mention an extra key to you, and she didn't mention you to me." She squirmed a little, then immediately wished she hadn't. "Uh, do you mind? Thanks," she murmured when he got to his feet.

"I'd say no problem if the damn room would stop spinning."

Still wary, Amara accepted the hand he held down to her. "Would you like me to look at your head?"

"Why?"

"Because you might have a concussion."

"That's a given, Red. I meant why you? Are you a doctor?"

"I'm a reconstructive surgeon."

"Seriously?" Laughing, he started for the back door. "You do face and butt lifts for a living?"

What had come perilously close to going hot and squishy inside her hardened. Her lips quirked into a cool smile. "There you go. Whatever pays the bills."

"If you say so."

She maintained her pleasant expression. "Returning to the omission thing… Can you think of any reason why Nana would neglect to mention you were living here when we talked?"

"You had a bad connection?"

Or more likely insufficient time to relate many details, thanks to Lieutenant Michaels, who'd done everything in his power, short of tearing the phone from her hand and tossing her into the backseat of his car, to hasten their departure. Amara glanced up as a gust of wind whistled through the rafters. "My mother would call this an omen and say I shouldn't have come."

"Yeah?" The cop—he'd said McVey, hadn't he?—picked up and tapped his iPhone as he wandered past the island. "She into the woo-woo stuff, too?"

"If by that you mean does she believe in some of the local legends? Absolutely."

He glanced at her. "There're more than two?"

"There are more than two hundred, but most of them are offshoots of the interconnected original pair. The Blumes are very big on their ancestor Hezekiah's transformation into a raven."

"I've noticed."

"That transformation is largely blamed on the Bellam witches."

"The Bellams being your ancestors."

"My grandmother's surname gave it away, huh?"

"Among other things. Setting the bulk of them aside and assuming you're Amara, your gran sent me a very short, very cryptic text message last night."

"You're just opening a text from last night now?"

"Give me a break, Red. It's my day off, this is my personal phone and the windstorm out there dislodged four shutters that I've spent the better part of the past twelve hours repairing and reattaching." He turned his iPhone so she could see the screen. "According to Grandma Bellam, you're in a whack of trouble from the crime lord you helped convict."

Amara read the message, then returned her gaze to his unfathomable and strangely compelling eyes. "*Whack* being the operative word. Look, it's late, and I'm intruding—apparently. I'm sure one of my aunts, uncles or cousins will put me up for the night." Wanting some distance between them, she started for the door. "I left my rental car at the foot of the driveway. It's pointed toward Raven's Hollow. As luck would have it, that's where my less antagonistic relatives live. So I'll leave you to whatever you were doing before we met and go break into one of their houses." She rummaged through her shoulder bag and produced the back door key. "I'll put this back under the flowerpot. Nana locks herself out at least three times a year."

Setting his phone on the island, McVey moved toward her. "Forget the key, Amara. Talk to me about this 'whack of trouble.'"

"It's a—sticky story."

"I'm a cop. I'm used to sticky. I'm also fine with 'sounds crazy,' if that helps."

It didn't. Neither did the fact that he'd ventured far enough into the light that she could see her initial assessment of him had been dead-on. The man was…well, gorgeous worked as well as any other word.

Long dark hair swept away from a pair of riveting brown eyes, and what female alive wouldn't kill for those cheekbones? Then there was the lean, rangy body. She wouldn't mind having that on top of her again…. And, God help her, where had that thought come from? She seriously needed to get her hormones under control, because no way should the idea of—okay, admit it—sex with an überhot man send her thoughts careening off to fantasyland.

Jimmy Sparks, vicious head of a family chock full of homicidal relatives, wanted her dead. She couldn't go back to New Orleans or her job, and she couldn't reasonably expect Lieutenant Michaels to do any more than he'd already done to help her. Her grandmother wasn't in Raven's Hollow, and Amara figured she'd probably alienated the Cove cop who was to the point where he might actually consider turning her over to Jimmy's kith and kin simply to be rid of her.

"I really am sorry about all of this." She backed toward the mudroom. "I wasn't expecting to find…"

"A wolf in Grandma's cottage?" He continued to advance. "Still waiting for the story, Red. If the trouble part's too big a leap, start with the 'less antagonistic relatives' reference."

"First off, I'd rather you called me Amara. You can see for yourself, my hair's more brown than red. Which, when you get right down to it, is the story of my relatives in an extremely simplified nutshell."

"Gonna need a bit more than that, I'm afraid. So far all I've got is that you're the descendant of a Bellam witch."

"Yes, but the question is which witch? Most Bellams

can trace the roots of their family tree back to Nola. There are only a handful of us who have her lesser-known sister Sarah's blood."

Finally, thankfully, he stopped moving. "If Nola and Sarah were sisters, what's the difference blood-wise?"

"Nola Bellam was married to Hezekiah Blume. At least she was, until Hezekiah went on a killing spree. According to the Blume legend, he repented. However, all those deaths got him turned into a clairvoyant raven. There wasn't a large window of opportunity for Nola to get pregnant. Unless you add in the unpleasant fact that Hezekiah's brother Ezekiel raped her, accused her of being a witch, then hunted her down and tried to destroy her. Thus, Hezekiah's killing spree."

"Complicated stuff."

"Isn't it? It gets worse, too, because, as luck would have it, sister Sarah had a thing for Ezekiel."

"And that 'thing' resulted in a child?"

"You catch on quick. Sarah had a daughter, who had a daughter and so on. So did Nola, of course, but not with Hezekiah. Even in legend, humans and ravens can't mate. Long story short, and rape notwithstanding, Nola never gave birth to a Blume baby. Sarah did." Amara shrugged. "I'm sure you know by now that Blumes and Bellams have been at odds for…well, ever. Raven's Cove versus Raven's Hollow in all things legendary and logical. So where does a Bellam with Blume blood in her background fit in? Does she cast spells or fall victim to them? And which town does she claim for her own? You can imagine the genetic dilemma."

McVey cocked his head. "You're not going to go all weird and spooky on me, are you?"

"Haven't got time for that, unfortunately."

"Knowing Jimmy Sparks, I tend to agree."

Her fingers froze on the doorknob. "You know him?"

"We've met once or twice." McVey sent her a casual smile. "Well, I say *met*, but it was really more a case of I shot at him."

"You fired bullets at Jimmy King-of-Grudges Sparks and lived to tell about it?"

"Put the living-to-tell part down to pure, dumb luck. I was painfully green at the time, but I was also a better shot than my partner, who took it upon himself through me to try to blow Sparks's tires out after we witnessed an illegal late-night exchange."

"And?"

"I hit two tires before someone inside the vehicle fired back. The shooter winged my partner. He got me in the shoulder, then got off when our report of the incident mysteriously disappeared. Before the night was done, we'd been ordered to forget the whole thing."

"Lucky Jimmy."

"Is that censure I hear in your voice, Red?"

"On the off chance that you actually do have a concussion, let's call it curiosity."

"Let's call it not your business, and move on to why one of this country's least-favorite sons is giving you, the descendant of a Maine witch, grief."

"I helped send him to prison. Seems my testimony pissed him off."

"Thereby landing you in a whack of trouble and leaving me with one last burning question." Without appearing to move, he closed the gap between them, wrapped his fingers and thumb lightly around her jaw and tipped her head back to stare down at her. "Why the hell has your witchy face been in my head for the past fifteen years?"

Chapter Four

He didn't expect an answer. He wasn't even sure why he'd asked the question. True, she looked very much like the woman in his recurring dream, but the longer he stared at her—couldn't help that part, unfortunately—the more the differences added up.

On closer inspection, Amara's hair really was more brown than red. Her features were also significantly finer than…whomever. Her gray eyes verged on charcoal, her slim curves were much better toned and her legs were the longest he'd seen on any woman anywhere.

He might have lingered on the last thing if she hadn't slapped a hand to his chest, narrowed those beautiful charcoal eyes to slits and seared him with a glare.

"What do you mean my face has been in your head for fifteen years? What the hell kind of question is that?"

A faint smile touched his lips. "Given my potentially concussed state, call it curiosity and forget I asked."

The suspicion returned. "Are you sure my grandmother's in the Caribbean and not locked in a closet upstairs?"

"This might not be the best time to be giving me ideas." With his eyes still on hers, he pulled a beeping iPhone from his pocket and pressed the speaker button. "What is it, Jake?"

"Got a problem here, Chief."

His deputy sounded stoked, which was never a good sign. But it was the background noises—the thumps, shouts and crashes—that told the story.

"Bar fight got out of hand, huh?"

"Wasn't my fault." Jake had to yell above the sound of shattering glass. "All I did was tell the witch people to mount their broomsticks and fly off home."

"You know you're in Raven's Hollow, right? Raven's Hollow, Bellam territory."

"Can I help it if folks in this town are touchy about their ancestors?"

"This night is deteriorating faster by the minute," McVey muttered.

Jake made a guttural sound as a fist struck someone's face. "Raven's Cove was settled first, and that's a fact. Why're you sticking up for a bunch of interlopers who can't hold their liquor and are proud of the fact that one of their stupid witch women made it so my great-great-whatever-granddaddy got turned into a bird?"

Were they actually having this conversation? McVey regarded Amara, who'd heard every word, and, holding her gaze, said calmly, "I'll be there in fifteen."

He could see she was trying not to laugh as he pocketed his phone and bent to retrieve the gun he'd lost during their scuffle.

"Sorry, but I did warn you, McVey."

"No, you didn't. You said your Raven's Hollow relatives represented the less antagonistic side of the family. That's not how Jake Blume's telling it."

"Twenty bucks says Jake started it."

Since that was entirely possible, McVey stuffed his weapon. "What can I say? He came with the job."

"The job's a powder keg, Chief, a fact that whoever

talked you into it obviously neglected to mention. Raven's Cove goes through police chiefs—"

"Like wolves go through grandmothers?" In a move intended to unsettle, he blocked her flight path. "Gonna need your keys, Red."

Unfazed, she ran her index finger over his chest. "Are you telling me, Chief McVey, that a deputy came with the job, but a vehicle didn't? Sounds like someone suckered you big time."

"I'm beginning to agree." And, damn it, get hot. "Keys are in case your car's closing my truck in. Knowing Jake as I do, we need to leave now."

"We?"

"You're coming with me."

"Excuse me?"

"Whack of trouble," he reminded her, and was relieved when she ground her teeth.

Their banter was getting way out of hand. Given the situation, a distraction like that that could turn into something bad very quickly.

He caught her shoulders before she could object, turned and nudged her through the mudroom. "As much as I'd love to argue this out, my instincts tell me you have a functioning brain and no particular desire to wait here alone for whatever family member Jimmy Sparks chooses to sic on you."

"I wasn't planning to wait anywhere."

"Right. You want to search for a place to flop in Raven's Hollow. At night, in a windstorm, with no idea how many of your relatives are home and how many are participating in the destruction of a Blume-owned bar at Harrow and Main in the Hollow."

"The Red Eye?" She laughed as he reached back to snag his badge from the table. "That's gonna piss Uncle Lazarus right off—assuming he still holds the lease on the place, which he will, seeing as he's notorious for acquiring properties and never selling them. Never selling anything, except possibly, like his ancestor Hezekiah, his soul."

"I'm getting that you don't like your uncle."

"It's not a question of like or dislike really. Uncle Lazarus is a miser and a misery of a man. He's also quite reclusive. Even so, your paths must have crossed a time or two since you arrived."

"More than a time or two, only once that mattered."

Wind whipped strands of long hair up into her face the moment they stepped onto the back porch. "What did you do, fine him for jaywalking?"

"Nope." McVey held the key ring in his mouth while he clipped the badge to his belt and checked his gun. "I arrested him for being drunk and disorderly."

Amara clawed the hair from her face. "I'm sorry. I thought you said he was drunk."

"He was hammered."

"And disorderly."

"He lurched into a dockside bar in Raven's Cove, staggered across the floor and slugged a delivery driver in the stomach." He pointed left. "My truck's that way."

"I see it. I'm waiting for the punch line."

"No line, just two punches. The second was a right uppercut to the driver's jaw. He's lucky the guy didn't file assault charges. I'd guess your uncle did a little boxing in his day."

"He did a lot of things in his day. But burst into Two Toes Joe's bar drunk? Not a chance." She hesitated. "Did he say why he did it?"

"Driver was a courier. He'd delivered a large padded envelope to your uncle's home in the north woods earlier that afternoon. Four hours later the guy's eyes were rolling back in his head. Lazarus pumped a fist, laughed like a lunatic and fell facedown on the floor."

"After which, you locked him in a jail cell."

"Yep."

"You put Lazarus Blume in jail and you're still in the Cove? Still chief of...? Hey, wait a minute." Already standing on the Ram truck's running board, she turned to jab a finger into his chest. "That is seriously not fair. I knew— I just knew he'd let a male get away with more than a female."

"What?"

"You heard me. You arrest him and nothing. No repercussions, no threats, no embellishing the whole suddenly sordid affair to your grandmother."

Okay, he was lost—and beginning to question her sanity. "What suddenly sordid affair?"

She poked him again. "I snuck out of my grandmother's house once, just once, so my friend and I could spy on her older sister's date with the local hottie, and wouldn't you know it, Uncle Lazarus spotted me. He dragged me back to Nana's and informed me I'd be mucking out his stable for the rest of the summer. Yet here you stand, still employed and without a speck of manure on your hands." She indicated herself, then him. "I'm a female, you're a male. It's not fair." Huffing out a breath, she sat, yanked the door closed and flopped back in her seat, arms folded. "I should have put two curses on him."

McVey climbed in beside her. "You put a— What did you do to him?"

She gave her fingers a casual flick. "What any self-respecting Bellam in my position would have done. I put a spell on the midnight snack Nana told me he always ate before going to bed. He had severe stomach cramps for the next three days. Some of my relatives swear they heard him laughing hysterically while the doctor was examining him. Other than cleaning his stables, I didn't hear or see him again for the rest of the summer. He'd always been a loner, but Nana told me he became even more of a phantom after his...spell of indigestion. I don't know if that's true or not. I was fourteen when it happened, and except for a mutual relative's funeral, our paths haven't crossed again."

McVey's lips quirked as he started the engine. "Note to self. Grudges run in your family."

She sent him a smoldering look. "Not a problem in your case, seeing as Uncle Lazarus's grudges don't appear to extend to men."

"I was referring to you, Red." The quirk of his lips became a full-fledged grin. "I'm not overly fond of stomach cramps."

On the heels of that remark, wind swooped down to batter the side of his truck. McVey heard a loud crack among the trees crowding the house and glanced upward.

"Stomach cramps will be the least of your problems if one of those evergreens destroys Nana's roof." As Amara spoke, the porch light went out then stuttered back on. "That's not good."

"Tell me something that is."

Overhead, a fierce gust of wind brought two large branches crashing down into the box of his truck.

"Dodgers probably lost by a landslide." He handed Amara his cell phone. "Do me a favor and speed-dial Jake. Tell him I'll need more than fifteen minutes."

"I can help you pull the branches from the—"

That was as far as she got before three shots rang out behind them.

She started to swing around, but McVey shoved her down and dragged the gun from his waistband. Keeping a hand on her neck, he risked a look, saw nothing and swore softly under his breath.

Amara pried his hand free. "Who is it?" she asked with barely a hint of a tremor.

"No idea. One of my backups is in the glove box. It's loaded. Use the keys." He gave the door a kick to open it. "Meanwhile, stay here and stay down. Unless you want to be pushing up daisies next to your Bellam and/or Blume ancestors."

"McVey, wait." She grabbed his arm. "I don't want you taking a bullet for me."

"Don't sweat it, Red." He risked a second look into the woods. "Chances are only fifty-fifty that those shots were fired by someone in Jimmy Sparks's family."

HE DISAPPEARED SO QUICKLY, Amara had no chance to ask what he meant. Or to wonder if she'd heard him correctly.

For a moment she simply stared after him and thought that somewhere along the line she must have fallen down a rabbit hole into a parallel universe where police chiefs looked like hot rock stars and any vestige of reality had long since been stripped away by a raging northeaster. Who was this stranger with the wicked sexy body and dark hypnotic eyes?

"More to the point," she said to her absent grandmother, "why didn't you mention him when I called you last night?"

Knowing she needed to think, Amara tucked the question away. Three bullets had just been fired at close range. A glance through the rear window revealed nothing except the moon, a scattering of stars and no flashlight beam. Actually—had McVey even taken a flashlight?

"I need you to step on it, Chief." Jake Blume's unexpected shout sent Amara's heart into her throat and almost caused her to drop the phone she'd speed-dialed without thinking. "You there, McVey?" the deputy yelled again. "Come on, what's taking you?"

"McVey's busy." As she spoke she pulled the key out of the ignition. "My name's Amara. We're still at Shirley Bellam's place."

"You fooling around with my superior officer out on the edge of the north woods ain't exactly my idea of help, sweetheart. Now, I don't give a rat's ass why you're in possession of McVey's phone. I just need you to put him on it." He waited a beat before adding a reluctant, "Please."

Amara tried one of the smaller keys in the glove box lock. "What you call fooling around, I call dodging bullets while your superior officer goes all Rambo and takes on an unidentified shooter in the woods. Trust me, his plate has more on it than yours does at the moment."

"Wanna bet?" The deputy's tight-lipped response gave way to a resounding punch. "You said Amara, right?" Another punch. "You wouldn't be that little witch bitch who used to come here in the summer, would you? Because if you are, you scared the bejesus out of my kid brother by telling him you could talk to ravens."

"Does it matter if I'm her?"

"Makes us cousins is all."

Since he practically spit the words out, Amara assumed the idea didn't sit well with him.

Behind her, three more shots rang out. She shoved another key into the lock—and breathed out in relief when the compartment popped open to reveal a 9 mm automatic. "Thank God."

"Depends on your point of view," Jake muttered. "As I recall, your last name's Bellam."

Irritated, she regarded the phone. "Did I mention someone's firing a rifle out here? I've counted six shots so far."

"Rifle shot, huh? Could be Owen thinking the sky's fixing to fall on his cabin. Old Owen ain't been right for years."

Parallel world, Amara reminded herself. "Will 'Old Owen' know the difference between McVey and a piece of falling sky?"

"I said it could be Owen," Jake countered. "It could just as easily be one of your backwoods cousins looking to shoot himself something feathered for the upcoming street barbecue."

Now she frowned at the phone. "You people are deranged."

She heard a grunt and a punch. "This from a raven whisperer?"

"I can't talk to—" She spun in place as three more shots sounded. "The whole world's deranged. Later, Deputy."

Tossing the phone aside, she firmed up her grip on McVey's gun and slid cautiously from the truck.

The wind blew in wild circles and made pinpointing the shooter's location next to impossible.

Amara searched the dark woods. Would Jimmy Sparks abandon all discretion this way? She didn't think so, but then, what did she know about the man's psyche? Maybe he'd sent a hothead after her.

Heart pounding, she worked her way along the side of the truck. She hissed in a breath when the tips of a broken branch snagged her hair like claws. She had to stop and untangle herself before she could continue.

Continue where, though, and do what when she got there? Her grandmother had taught her how to shoot clay pigeons, but she doubted the owner of the rifle would move in a high, wide arc for her.

"What the hell are you doing?"

The question came from close behind her. Snapping the

gun up, Amara spun on one knee and almost—almost—squeezed the trigger.

When she saw who it was, her vision hazed and she lowered her arms. "Jesus, McVey."

"Have you gone mad?"

"Don't you dare glare at me. I counted nine shots, none of which came from a handgun. For all I know, you could've been dead or bleeding to death in the woods."

"I also could've shot you in the back. You want to protect yourself, you use the best cover you've got. Case in point, my truck."

"I'll remember that next time someone decides to fire a rifle in the middle of nowhere, during a windstorm, while a cop with a much bigger weapon than the one he left behind disregards his own advice and takes off in pursuit." Pushing aside the hand he held out to her, she stood and dusted off her jeans. "I talked to your deputy while you were gone. He seems to think the rifleman might be someone called Owen, worried that the sky's falling."

McVey ran his gaze around the clearing. "It wasn't Owen."

"Figured not. A Bellam bird hunter was his second suggestion. Looking for barbecue night's winged entrée."

"Red, the most common birds in these woods at night are owls, and not even a grill can make a screech owl taste good."

Moving her lips into a smile, Amara dropped the gun into his free hand. "I keep telling myself that at some point this night will end. Whether any part of it makes sense when it does remains to be seen. Moving on, if not Owen or someone who likes to hunt owls, are we back to a member of the Sparks family as the prospective shooter?"

He kept scanning. "Not necessarily."

"Didn't think so."

"Yeah, you did, but think deeper. Sparks wouldn't want you taken out in such an obvious fashion. It's true, Jimmy has moments of blind rage during which he loses all control, but that's the reason he gets people with cooler heads to do his dirty work."

"There's good news. Look, McVey, if you think the shooter's close enough to be watching us, why are we standing here having his discussion?"

"Shooter's gone." He made a final sweep before bringing his eyes back to hers. "If he wasn't, we'd be dead."

Spreading her fingers, she gave a humorless laugh. "I am so out of my element right now. Is there any chance you're going to tell me what you think just happened here?"

"Someone fired a rifle nine times, then took off."

"And you know he's gone because…?"

"I heard his truck."

"Are you—?"

She saw him move, but not in time to avoid the fingers that curled around the nape of her neck.

He stared down at her. "The only thing I'm sure of, Amara, is that we need to get something out of the way before it gets both of us killed."

"What? No." With the truck at her back, she had nowhere to go, no escape. "Don't you dare do this, McVey. I'm messed up enough already without adding sex to the mix."

A dangerous grin appeared. "I wasn't thinking sex quite yet, Red, but I could probably be persuaded."

She planted her palms firmly on his chest. "You're messing with my mind." And tangling everything inside her into a hot ball of… She wasn't sure what, but something that wanted very badly to take things a whole lot deeper a whole lot faster than she should.

"Lady, you've been messing with my mind for fifteen years."

"Don't go there."

"Not planning to." Eyes gleaming, he lowered his head until his mouth hovered a tantalizing inch above hers. "If you really want to stop me, Red, this is your last chance."

"Seriously, McVey. We shouldn't… I'm not…" She exhaled heavily. "I hate you." Casting caution to the still-howling wind, Amara took his face in her hands and yanked his very sexy mouth down onto hers.

LIEUTENANT ARTHUR MICHAELS mopped the back of his neck as he climbed the stairs to his Algiers apartment. He'd taken a roundabout route from Jackson, Mississippi, to New Orleans—by way of Arkansas and an old friend, who'd given him both a bed for the night and a name: Willy Sparks.

Rumor had it Willy could outthink a fox, outmaneuver a weasel and poison an enemy so neatly that the best forensic teams in the country were left scratching their collective heads as to why the corpse they were examining didn't simply get up and walk out of the room.

And speaking of rooms… He saw right away that the door to his apartment was still marked with the tiny paper he'd placed between it and the frame before leaving town. Absurdly relieved, he went inside, shed his jacket and cranked the high windows open.

One of his neighbors was having a party. Boisterous jazz, led by trumpet and saxophone, drifted through the openings. The smell of gumbo made his mouth water and his system long for a cold beer. Being a cautious man, however, he settled for water from the jug in his fridge.

He didn't hear the sound behind him as much as sense it in the light brush of air on his neck.

It only took him a split second to unholster his gun, spin and aim at— Nothing, he realized. Funny, he could have sworn…

Several rapid eyeblinks later, he lowered his arm.

He continued to blink as the edges of the apartment fuzzed. His fingers lost sensation. The gun clattered to the floor.

"Son of a…"

"Ah, ah, ah." One of the long shadows came alive in the form of a wagging finger. "Don't be rude, Lieutenant, or I'll go against orders and add unspeakable pain to your death. It's a well-known fact that Willy Sparks's mother is not what you were just about to call her."

He couldn't move, Michaels realized; not anything except his eyes.

He slumped to the floor. Hands groped his pockets, then rolled him onto this back like a discarded doll. He heard a series of beeps beneath his neighbor's music. When they stopped, a low chuckle floated downward.

"You have a most obliging BlackBerry. Raven's Hollow, Maine. That's very far north, isn't it? But you know, Lieutenant, I've heard the water's much safer to drink up in Maine than it is here in the Big Easy."

The BlackBerry hit the floor. Water gurgled down the drain. The music played on. His apartment door clicked shut. And Lieutenant Arthur Michaels thought of ravens….

Chapter Five

Lock it away, Amara cautioned herself. Bring it out later—because how could she not? But she'd kissed men before and would again, so...not a problem.

Unless she acknowledged the fact that ten minutes after she'd dragged her mouth from his, her senses continued to zap like an electric wire gone wild.

Did McVey feel the same? They were in his truck, driving. She couldn't read his profile, and he hadn't really looked at her or talked to her, so who knew?

There was that other thing, too; the part about her face having been in his head for fifteen years. What was she supposed to do with that weird knowledge?

He finally glanced over as they neared the outskirts of the Hollow. "You're annoyed, aren't you, Red? I can feel the vibes taking bites out of me."

Amara flicked him a similar look. "Don't flatter yourself, McVey. It's been a very bizarre night. I was torn between kissing you and kneeing you. It just so happens I'm a pacifist."

"Is that why I have four gouges in my left cheek?"

"You tackled me in my grandmother's house. Maybe you're renting it at the moment, but I didn't know that going in."

"Breaking in."

Her lips curved. "I'm fairly certain that using a key to enter a property can't be construed as a break-in. However, to answer your question, yes, I'm annoyed, just not for the reason you probably think." Lowering the visor, she regarded the tangled mess of her hair, sighed and began rooting through her shoulder bag for a brush. "I liked it."

"I know."

She heard the amusement in his tone and told herself not to react. "I know you know. That's why I'm annoyed. Tell me—" she worked the brush through the tangles "—do you eat midnight snacks?"

"Not anymore." He swung onto Main Street, made a wide U-turn and stopped in a no-parking zone. "You might want to stay behind me when we go inside. I see two broken windows."

"I see four. I hope whoever broke them likes mucking out stables. Male or female, when it comes to serious property damage, Uncle Lazarus is a tyrant."

"You know your family's a little scary, right?"

"Which side?"

"Take your pick," he said as they approached the front door. "Now, unless your repertoire contains a curse for every occasion, remember to stick close when we go in."

Low lights tinged with red burned throughout the bar. Kiss rocked the jukebox and glass crunched like pebbles underfoot. Oh, yeah, Amara thought, Uncle Lazarus would be plenty pissed.

To the left of the entryway, behind a long line of pool tables, a dozen broken chairs and tables sat in a cockeyed heap. Groups of customers continued to hurl insults back and forth across the remaining tables. Amara spotted more than a few drops of blood both on the people and on the floor.

"Well, hallelujah, Chief, you made it." A tall man with

receding brown hair, heavy stubble and bean-black eyes pushed through the crowd. He wore a tan T-shirt, a shoulder holster and a frown that became a sneer when he spied his newly arrived Bellam cousin.

"Spit and I'll suspend you," McVey warned, not looking at him. "I assume you two have met."

"I know who she is." A muscle twitched in Jake's jaw. "She don't look much different than she did the night she gave my brother Jimbo the screaming meemies up on Raven's Ridge."

"I imagine that was unintentional, Deputy."

As a wave of people began to enfold him, Amara shrugged. "It wasn't, actually. I meant to scare him, and it worked."

"Jimbo was a year and a half younger than you," Jake accused.

"He was also forty pounds heavier, six inches taller and trying very hard to coax me into jumping off the edge of the cliff."

"You could've said no."

"He said he didn't like that word. *Push,* though…he liked that word a lot."

Jake thrust his chin out. "He was a kid."

"So was I."

"He still half believes one of his spooky Bellam cousins can talk to ravens and make them do her bidding. Frigging witch."

Losing patience, Amara regarded him through her lashes. "Don't tempt me. I'm older now and less…tolerant."

Jake showed his teeth but didn't, she noticed, utter another word.

"Smart man." Through a crowd that was now vying loudly for his attention, McVey indicated the carnage in the corner. "How many arrests have you made?"

Jake dragged his resentful gaze from Amara. "Six. When you didn't show, I called the Hardens in to help out."

"Part-time Hollow deputies," McVey said over his shoulder. "Twins."

"Thick as bricks, the pair of them." Jake snarled at a trio of men who elbowed him aside and began pleading their cases to McVey. "The Hardens are kin to Tyler Blume. No idea why he took the job, but Tyler's the police chief here in the Hollow." He raised his voice. "A town we Cove cops are being forced to watch over while he's off snorkeling with his new Bellam wife."

"That would be my cousin Molly." When McVey shifted his attention from the squabbling men to arch a brow in Amara's direction, she let her eyes sparkle. "It gets complicated very quickly if you start talking relatives around here. Think of me and Nana as the link between two feuding families." Without missing a beat, she offered a placid, "Say *missing link,* Jake, and you'll have hemorrhoids by the end of your shift."

She felt the deputy's glare before he pushed his way to McVey's other side.

A man with a pockmarked face and no neck shouted over Amara's head, "Was a Blume who started it, McVey. Called our beer donkey—er, well, anyway, he accused Yolanda of cutting it."

Amara poked McVey's hip. "Does Yolanda Bellam manage this bar?"

"More or less…. Yeah, Frank, I heard you…. From your expression, I'd speculate you and Yolanda aren't BFFs."

"Put it this way, if I'd known she was here, I'd have taken my chances with the shooter up at Nana's."

On cue, a high female voice sliced through the predominately male grumbles. "Amara? My God, is it really you?"

Her cousin had a little-girl drawl, glossy pink lips and

red-blond curls clipped back at the sides to show off her angelic face.

Yeah, right, angelic, Amara thought, tipping her lips into a smile as a pair of wide blue eyes joined the mix. "Hey, Yolanda. It's been— Well, years."

Her cousin pushed a man out of her path, slung the dish towel she carried over her shoulder and spread her arms in welcome.

"Cousin Ammie's back. And isn't she a living doll? She brought me the best present ever." Those welcoming arms knocked Amara aside and wrapped themselves tightly around McVey's neck. "How's the handsomest lawman on the East Coast tonight?" Her eyes and mouth grew suddenly tragic. "You'll make them pay, won't you, McVey? I tried, but I couldn't get any such promise out of your mean-mouthed deputy."

Amara's opinion of Jake shot up ten full points. She wasn't so sure about McVey.

To his credit, however, he removed her clinging arms, sent Amara a humorous look and headed for the pool tables, where three men with pierced body parts were holding their cues like baseball bats.

Yolanda pouted after him…until someone stepped on her foot and then the pout became a snarl. "You still nipping chins and lifting butts?"

Unruffled, Amara smiled. "Why? Are you looking for a freebie?"

"I wouldn't come to you if I was."

"Only because we apply the word in different ways."

Yolanda's fists balled. "I could blacken both your eyes, you know."

"I'd say the same, except you've already done it yourself."

"I— Damn!" Wiping a finger under her lower lashes,

Yolanda scowled. "Some dumb Blume threw a beer and got me square in the face." She gave her other eye a wipe. "Talk to me, Amara. Why have you come here after fifteen years of not here?"

"I wanted to see Nana."

"In that case, Portland's an hour's drive south and have a nice flight. Nana's in St. Croix. Or maybe it's the Cayman Islands. Anyway, you'll find her if you look hard enough." With the speed of a striking snake, she grabbed Amara's trench coat and yanked her forward to hiss, "He's mine. You got that?"

Amara pried her hand away. "I got it when you turned into a barnacle a minute ago."

Her cousin's eyes flashed. "I can make your life hell."

"You can try." And, she admitted silently, might have succeeded if Jimmy Sparks hadn't beaten her to it. "In an effort to keep the peace, Yolanda, if McVey says he's yours, he's yours. And welcome to you."

A finger jabbed her shoulder. "You can't stay at Nana's house while you're here."

"Yep, figured that one out, too."

"Can't stay with me and Larry, either."

"Your brother, Larry, the nighttime nudist? Uh, no."

The overhead lights surged and faded and caused an icy finger to slide along Amara's spine.

"Stupid wind." But Yolanda observed her more keenly now. "A little raven told me you had some heavy court action going on down south. Saw someone die who wasn't on your operating table when it happened."

She didn't need this, Amara thought, but rather than snap at her cousin, she shrugged it off. "I saw. I testified. It's done." When the lights faded again, she added a quick, "Uh, how's Uncle Lazarus?"

Yolanda sniffed. "Still pays me next to nothing to manage this rude branch of hell, but he's a Blume, so what do you expect?" Her lips quirked. "Word is the man you testified against is the mean and powerful head of a family that's into all sorts of nasty things. Extortion, weapons, drugs—murder."

"My, what big ears you have, Grandma." His pool-player problems apparently dealt with, McVey surprised Amara by dropping an arm over her shoulders. "Some analogies go on forever, don't they, Red?" Before she could answer, he made a head motion at the crowd. "I'm seeing a lot of unfamiliar faces, Yolanda. They drifting in for the Night of the Raven Festival already?"

Amara knew her cheeks went pale. She glanced at a nonexistent watch on her wrist, then at the walls for a calendar. "Is it—? What's today? The date," she clarified, still searching.

"May 10," McVey supplied. "Why?"

"What? Oh, nothing. I forgot…an appointment."

But damn, damn, how on earth had she forgotten about the scores of strangers who drove, bussed, cycled and hitchhiked to Raven's Hollow to take part in the three-day celebration known as the Night of the Raven?

The Night festival was the Hollow's once-a-year answer to the Cove's once-every-three-years Ravenspell. Although the story at the root of the events was the same, it was told from two very different perspectives. Over the years both events—the Cove's in the fall and the Hollow's in the spring—had become a magnet for every curse-loving fanatic in and out of the state.

This was, Amara realized, the worst possible time for her to be in either town.

Her smile nothing short of malicious, Yolanda drew a raven's head in the residue of a spilled beer. "Bet the Cayman Islands are looking better and better about now, huh,

Amara? Say the word and I'll get right on my little computer and book you a flight out of Portland."

When a shrill whistle cut through the crowd noise, she banged her fist on the bar. "I'm not a dog, Jake Blume. What do you want?"

He wagged the receiver of a corded wall phone. "Boss man's on the line and he's in a crappy mood."

"I hate that man," Yolanda breathed. "Both men. Remember the spiders, Amara." With a lethal look for her cousin, she snapped the dish towel from her shoulder and vanished into a sea of bodies.

"She put a jar of them in my bed," Amara said before McVey could ask. "Well, I say *she*, but Yolanda only had the idea. Jake and Larry collected and planted them."

"In your bed."

"Under the covers, at the bottom. She told them to leave the top off so the spiders could crawl around wherever. The things were big. I freaked and refused to sleep in that particular room again."

McVey tugged on a strand of hair to tilt her head back. "Did you tell your grandmother?"

"No need."

"Do I want to know why?"

"Because all three of them, Jake most particularly, are terrified of snakes." She swept an arm around the room. "Is the fighting done?"

"For now." He nodded at a row of dull brass taps that glowed an eerie shade of red under lights that continued to surge and fade. "Do you want a drink before we leave?"

"Poison is a witch's weapon, McVey, and Yolanda's a Bellam. But thanks for the offer."

"Festival slipped your mind, didn't it?"

She ran her hands up and down her arms. "Unfortunately. The prospect of eminent death must have pushed it out. I've only ever been to one Night celebration my-self. If it's of any interest to you—and it should be—the Hollow's Night of the Raven isn't quite as civilized as the Cove's Ravenspell."

"Translation, Tyler Blume deliberately planned his hon-eymoon so he'd miss it."

"If you've met him, you know he did. On the other hand, Jake should be in his element." She glanced up when the lights winked off. "Uh…" Then back on. "Okay, my nerves are getting a way bigger workout than they need."

She heard a familiar double beep beneath wailing Tim McGraw. As she hunted in her shoulder bag for her phone, she saw McVey pluck a mug of beer from a much larger man's hand.

"You're over your limit, Samson. Unless you want to join your buddies in jail, go home."

The man's face reddened. "Gonna get my wife to put a pox on you, you don't give that back, McVey."

"Do it, and I'll get Red here to put one on you."

"My wife's got an aunt who's a Bellam." The man jerked his stubbly chin. "What's she got?"

Staring at her iPhone, Amara felt her brain go cold. What she had was a text message from a man who'd sworn he would only contact her in an emergency.

"Beat it, Samson."

Giving the mug to the bartender, McVey turned her hand with the iPhone and read the name on the screen. A name Amara's terrified mind didn't want to see or to acknowledge. Willy Sparks.

SHE PACED THE back office of the Raven's Hollow police station like a caged tiger, dialing and redialing her cell. At the front desk Jake muttered about the Harden brothers being allowed to go home while he had to ride herd on a bunch of drunks in a town that wasn't his and didn't even supply its officers with a decent coffeemaker.

On his side of things, McVey was seriously wishing he'd never made any kind of deathbed promise to his father. Raising his eyes, he watched Amara pace. Okay, maybe not so much wishing as wondering what the hell he was supposed to do with this mess.

"Come on, McVey, give me one good reason why I can't haul these boozers to the Cove. Cells there are way more comfortable than here."

McVey scrolled through a list of New Orleans police officers. "Paperwork, Jake. Triple the usual amount if we start shuffling prisoners around. And you'll be doing every last bit of it."

The deputy gave his rifle a resentful pump. "I could get me a job in Bangor, you know."

"Any time you want that to happen…" A raven-shaped wall clock told McVey he'd been on his iPhone for more than forty minutes. Out of patience, he took a procedural shortcut to a friend of a friend on the New Orleans force. "Samson's texted me three times since we left the Red Eye," he said absently. "Wants me to pay for the beer he didn't get to drink."

Amara kept pacing. "Sounds as though Samson's spent some time around Uncle Lazarus…. There's still no answer at the lieutenant's apartment, McVey. I've tried his BlackBerry and his landline a dozen times each."

McVey flicked her a look but said nothing. Didn't need to; she knew the score as well as he did.

It took the better part of an hour to connect with someone in a position of sufficient authority to have Michaels's apartment checked out. Another hour and a blistering headache later, the captain from the lieutenant's parish contacted him personally.

"Michaels is dead." The man's tone was lifeless, a condition McVey understood all too well. "Officers found him on his back, staring at the ceiling. He had both hands clamped around his BlackBerry."

"Cause of death?"

"Given the situation, I'd go with some kind of off-the-radar toxin that simulates a stroke. Forensic team's scouring the apartment as we speak. I'll let you know what they turn up."

Amara rubbed her forehead with her own phone after the captain signed off. "Michaels is dead because he helped me get out of New Orleans. This is my fault."

Figuring sympathy wasn't the way to go here, McVey countered with a bland, "You know that's a load of bull, right? And if we all just went with it, Willy Sparks would go on killing cops and civilians ad infinitum."

She shot him a vexed look. "Thanks for the shoulder."

"You don't want a shoulder, Amara. You want to pound your fists. If I tell you it's not your fault, you'll get angry and say it should've been you, because that's who Jimmy Sparks was gunning for."

"He was. He is. And as emotional releases go, angry words are better than furious fists."

"Not always. Back on point, what if Sparks's nephew, godson, second cousin—whatever—had killed you instead of Michaels. Then what? True, he'd get paid, maybe bask on a tropical island for a while, but what he'd really be doing is waiting for Uncle Jimmy to crook his finger again and point it at a new target. The way things stand, this job's not done. In fact, it's a good bet Willy Sparks is either en route to or has already arrived in whatever Raven town the lieutenant entered into his BlackBerry."

Amara frowned at her cell, then at him. "He said he buried the destination and phone number."

"There's buried, and there's buried, Red. The phone wasn't taken, therefore there was no need to take it."

"As in the killer got what he wanted from it before he left." She closed her eyes. "My ex is a geek. He could hack into just about any device."

"Geeks can murder as effectively as anyone, Amara."

"So it seems." She looked around the office. "I need to leave before he gets here."

McVey regarded his iPhone screen, shook his head and pushed off from the windowsill where he'd been leaning. "You're not getting this, are you? Skip past the beating-yourself-up part, Amara, and think."

"I'm not beating myself...well, yes, I am, but that's because I feel responsible."

"Did you kill him?"

"You're joking, right? I'm a doctor, McVey. Psychology doesn't work on me."

"Fine. Here's the reality. You leave town, Willy arrives. He's pissed off to start with. Then he stops and thinks. And being a pro, sees a golden opportunity to draw you back."

"By hurting members of my family."

"Wouldn't you, in his position?"

"Let me think. Uh—no."

"Put your mind in his. We're talking about a killer here." When she didn't respond, McVey held his arms out to the sides. "Look, if it'll help get you past the guilt and make you see reason, you're welcome to take your best physical shot. All I want in return is a handful of Tylenols, a couple hours of sleep and no argument from you about where you'll be spending the night. You have two options. Come with me to your grandmother's place or hang with Jake on a cot in the back room."

"That's quite a choice. Seeing as I know all the hidey-holes at Nana's house and wouldn't trust Jake not to sell me out for cab fare, I'll go with the lesser evil and take you. As for the gut punch, I'll take a rain check."

"Excellent choices," McVey returned.

Although it felt like a betrayal of sorts, he deliberately neglected to tell her about the text message Michaels's captain had sent him less than a minute ago. But it continued to play in his head like a stuck audio disk.

In the captain's opinion, if one of his most experienced detectives could be taken out as easily as Michaels apparently had been, then it was only a matter of time—likely short—before the fourth person on Jimmy Sparks's hit list followed him to the grave.

Chapter Six

If you believed local lore, the wind on Hollow Road was an echo of Sarah Bellam's dying wail. A final protest, Amara supposed, against the unfair hand she believed she'd been dealt.

As a child, Amara had loved hearing stories about Sarah. As an adult—well, suffice it to say the last place she wanted to be was on a twisty, turny, extremely narrow strip of pavement that wound an impossible path to the edge of the north woods, listening to the wind howl like a raging witch.

She glanced out and up as the road forked. The left side made a steep and treacherous climb to the imposing structure that was Bellam Manor. The first time she'd seen it at four years of age, all the Gothic points, tall gables and arrow-slatted windows had struck her as extremely castle-like. Bad castle, not good. This was where Sarah had been born, raised and, most agreed, confined for the final years of her life. The locals of the day had branded her evil, and the description had stuck.

The same description could be applied to Jimmy Sparks. Unfortunately, even in prison, Sparks wielded sufficient power to have people murdered.

The picture of Lieutenant Michaels's face that swam into Amara's head caused pain to spike and spread. Had he died because of her, or had Jimmy Sparks wanted him gone in any case? Would she ever know? Would it make a difference if she did?

"So, Red, is it the wind, Michaels's death or me that's bothering you?"

McVey's question shattered the beginnings of a dreadful memory. Amara pressed on a nerve at the side of her neck. "The death's the worst. But as we get farther and farther from so-called civilization, I am starting to wonder why you've taken such an active interest in my welfare."

A smile grazed his lips. "It's my job to be interested, isn't it?"

"It's not your job to play personal watchdog. You could have fobbed me off to any number of relatives, including Yolanda and her extremely strange brother, Larry."

"The sleepwalking streaker who spends his winters working at a Colorado ski resort?"

"He's part of an avalanche control team. Helps bring the snow down before it gets too deep and dangerous. Nana said he wound up in the hospital with frostbite after one of his naked nighttime walks. I guess he knows his way around plastic explosives. Have you met him?"

"Several times. Four of them at night."

"That's unfortunate. But it doesn't answer my earlier question."

"Yeah, it does. I don't fob people off. And I'm definitely not a sadist."

"You're something, though, aren't you?" Tucking a leg up, Amara turned to study him. "Something not what or who people think you are."

His smile widened and caused a shiver of excitement to dance along her spine. "You're fishing, Red. I'm not biting."

"You don't have to. You gave it away when you told me

there was only a fifty-fifty chance the shots we heard at Nana's were fired by someone in Jimmy Sparks's family. What's the flip side, McVey? What or who represents the other fifty percent?"

"Could be I have an angry ex."

"Could also be Yolanda and I will develop a sisterly affection for each other. But back in the real world, what aren't you telling me about those shots? We heard nine of them, in three groups of three. Is the number significant? Is it connected to the fact that you think my face has been in your head for fifteen years—which, by the way, is exactly how long it's been since the last time I was in the Hollow."

"Yeah?" He glanced at her again.

"Fifteen years this June."

"Huh."

She sighed. "Please don't go all dark and mysterious on me."

He regarded the towering trees through the upper portion of the windshield. "I asked a simple question, Red. Right now I'm just trying to keep my truck on the road."

"And I'm trying to figure out if I'm riding with a man or someone who was hatched from an alien pod. Call me anal, but informing me I have the same face as some woman in your head isn't your usual 'first time we've met' remark. Assuming, of course, this is the first time we've met."

"I did meet a beautiful redhead at the tail end of a wedding reception a few years back. Her features are a bit of a blur at this point, but I remember thinking she was gorgeous. The reception was in Albany. I was the guy playing the air guitar—with a little help from Keith Richards."

She fought back a laugh. "Don't do this, McVey. It's been a very long, very weird night, to say nothing of sad." A picture of Yolanda popped in. "And irritating."

He looked at her for a thoughtful moment. "You're part

of a dream, Amara. A nightmare, actually. One I've had off and on since I was nineteen."

"Ah, well, that clears things right up, doesn't it—seeing as we're total strangers." Her expression grew wary. "You're not a Bellam somewhere in that dark and mysterious past of yours, are you?"

"If I am, it'll be a hard thing to prove. I'm what's called a foundling. Or close enough that the term applies."

Sympathy softened everything inside her. "I'm so sorry, McVey. Were you adopted?"

"In a sense."

"You know that answer's a form of avoidance, don't you?"

"I know it's the best you're going to get right now. As for me seeing your face, I dream what I dream, and believe me when I tell you, I don't enjoy the experience."

"Well, that's me flattered."

"You're a hag in the opening act."

"Better and better."

"You come into my head chanting over a fire in a room filled with smoke. Next thing I know, you've sent a man God knows where and you're telling me you intend to take my memories away. And, hell, maybe you pulled it off, because the dream ends there every damn time I have it."

A pinecone bounced off the windshield, catching Amara's gaze. "I'm sliding very quickly across the line to freaked, McVey. I'm not responsible for your dreams. I don't chant over fires or zap memories from men's minds or—"

"I'm not a man in the dream."

"Boys' minds, then… Whoa!" She braced herself with both hands as a blast of wind punched the truck like a giant fist.

McVey glanced skyward. "If there's anything in your

background that can affect the elements, Red, now would be a really good time to call on it."

"I've never actually… Oh, my God, is that the yellow-ribbon tree?" Shocked, she stared at the huge, uprooted oak that currently lay between her grandmother's house and one of the outbuildings. "It was a hundred and twenty years old."

"It missed the roof by less than five feet." McVey pulled into the driveway. "It also flattened the old well." With his eyes on the exposed roots, he reached for his beeping cell. "What is it, Jake?"

Amara slid from the truck while he talked to his deputy. Some of the branches had scraped the outer wall of the house. Thank God her grandmother hadn't been inside at the time.

Still on his phone, McVey headed over to survey the damage. Amara left him to it and turned for her rental car. She needed at least one of her suitcases and she wanted her medical kit. It might not be smart for her to touch McVey given their earlier wow of a kiss, but as she'd put the scratches on his cheek, she felt she owed it to him to clean them up.

Score settled. Or as settled as it could be with lust doing its best to tie her in knots.

She scooped the hair from her face as she approached the vehicle. "Dozens of so-called witches in Raven's Hollow, yet no one's moved this stupid wind along." She shot a vexed look at the night sky. "I'm sure Bangor could use a good airing out."

The wind shrieked in response and almost caused her to stumble into the driver's-side door.

"I'll take that as a no."

Releasing her hair, Amara reached for the handle. And froze with her fingers mere inches away.

Her throat dried up. "Uh, McVey?"

Of course he couldn't hear her. She could barely hear herself. But she could see. And what she saw was a man. He was slumped over the steering wheel of her rental car. Long blond hair obscured his features, but he wore a sleeveless shirt and, most significant to Amara, he wasn't moving.

"McVey?" She inched closer. Was he breathing?

"McVey!" she called again. When the man failed to stir, she took a bolstering breath and opened the door.

His head came up lightning-fast. His eyes glinted. "Hello, gorgeous." He offered a freakish smile, whipped his right hand around and gave his wrist a double flick. Amara saw the gleam of a knife a split second before she turned and bolted.

Thoughts scrambled in her head. Had there been blood on the blade? On him? Pretty sure she'd seen red streaks on his arms.

Trees and bushes rushed past in a blur. There it was, the lit porch of her grandmother's house, less than fifty feet away. "McVey!"

Suddenly the porch light winked out. Everything around her went dark. Amara stepped on a fallen branch and had to slow down. "Ouch! McVey!"

A man's hands descended on her shoulders from behind.

She didn't think or hesitate. She simply spun, knocked the hands away and brought her knee up hard.

She heard a cursed reaction.

"Are you insane? Amara, it's me."

McVey swung her around so they were back to front, holding her in place with a forearm pressed lightly across her throat. "Have you lost your mind?"

She pointed straight ahead. "Man. In my car. With a

knife." Her fingernails sank into his wrist. "There might be blood."

McVey released her. "Stay here."

"What? No. Now who's insane? He could be anywhere."

"Fine. Stay behind me."

She did. Unfortunately she was so close behind that she collided with his back when he halted.

He said nothing, just passed her a penlight from his pocket and pressed a hand to her stomach to keep her in place. He had his gun out, but as it was aimed at the ground, she understood even before she angled the light at the car.

The man inside had vanished.

"I AM SO done with this night," Amara declared.

McVey followed her around the fallen tree and across the yard to the porch. Thankfully, the generator had kicked in.

"I want to believe the guy I saw was your resident nutball taking refuge from the falling sky, but the Crocodile Dundee knife suggests…well…not." He saw her shoulders hunch. "Do you have any theories?"

"None worth mentioning."

"Figures." When she turned for a last look behind them, he felt her eyes on his cheek. "And then there's this." A sigh escaped. "They're not deep scratches, but I bet they sting." Lifting a hand, she used her index finger to draw a circle. "They should heal fast enough."

"They always do."

Smiling a little, she drew another circle. "Meaning you've been scratched before?"

"I worked in vice in Chicago. Cops get scratched, punched, kicked and shot at on a regular basis."

"I guess the Hollow's a cakewalk by comparison."

"Depends on your definition of the term. I've been scratched, kicked and shot at within the space of five hours tonight."

"Pretty sure Samson was thinking about punching you at the Red Eye." Her eyes danced. "You're four for four, Chief, and the Night of the Raven hasn't even begun."

"Maybe I should have gone to Florida with Tyler and Molly."

"You still can."

He dropped his gaze briefly to her mouth. "No, I really can't." Wouldn't if he could. And, God help him, he had no desire to explore that scary-as-hell thought.

She circled the scratches a third time and then let her hand fall away.

Was it crazy that, for a single blind moment, he wanted to abandon all logic and have wild sex with her on the kitchen floor? His hormones said no. Fortunately for both of them, his brain retained control.

"You should go upstairs," he said before the badly frayed threads of his restraint snapped and he turned into the big bad wolf they'd been playing with all night.

He started to step back. Then blew his good intentions to hell and covered her mouth with his.

For the first time in memory the world around him dissolved, leaving him with nothing except the full-bodied taste of woman and the mildly unnerving sensation that some small part of her was seeping into his bloodstream like a drug. Whether good or bad, he couldn't say. He only knew his control currently teetered on a very ragged edge. Drawing on the dregs of it, he gripped her arms and set her away from him.

"Well, wow." Amara fingered her lips. Her eyes had gone a fascinating shade of silver. "That was…amazing. I don't normally kiss men I've just met like that. Not altogether sure I've kissed any man like that." She bit lightly on her lower lip. "You?"

"I try not to kiss men at all if I can avoid it."

She laughed, and that didn't help a damn thing. "No Irish or Italian in your background, hmm?"

He fixed his gaze on hers. "You want to go upstairs, Amara, now, before it occurs to me that self-restraint's never been my best quality."

A sparkle lit her eyes. Tugging him forward by his shirt, she whispered a teasing "Mine, either."

He let her stroll away. This might be Grandma's house, but he hadn't regressed to a wild-animal state quite yet.

Rifle shots, he reminded himself. Supersize knife. Twisted leer. Oh, yeah, that worked. Anticipation rose. Adrenaline ramped it up.

He gave Amara sixty minutes to settle in—and his libido the same amount of time to settle down. Then he checked his guns, pulled on a dark jacket and made himself part of the night.

Location presented no problem. He'd discovered several spent cartridges earlier in a section of the woods where three giant oak trees stood bent and tortured around a collection of boulders that resembled witches' hats.

A silent approach wasn't necessary. The wind raged on—like a huffing, puffing wolf, if he wanted to keep the fairy tale alive a bit longer.

He reached the clearing within fifteen minutes. Playing his flashlight over the tops of the stone hats, he let a wry smile form. Despite the whirling gusts, he clearly caught the sound of a rifle being primed.

Sticking to the shadows, he called, "You want to shoot me, Westor, do it now. I don't play mind games these days."

"Like hell." The reply came from a patch of darkness some fifty feet to McVey's left. "You've been playing with minds in two freaking—and I gotta say freaky—towns for more than a year. I did some sniffing around tonight, old friend. You've got these people believing you're a man of honor, someone who'll stand up for them should the need arise. But you and me, we know different, don't we? You'd sell your granny, if you had one, for the gold fillings in her teeth. You'd sell me, if you could, for a whole lot less."

"Or I could just keep it simple and arrest you for shooting at my landlady's granddaughter."

"In that case, I might as well kill her and let the chips fall. A little bird told me she's got majorly big problems that'll land her six feet under before long anyway."

"Raven." McVey scanned the darkness. "It's all about big black ravens around here."

"Ravens and witches is how I heard it."

"From your little bird?"

Westor Hall gave his rifle another Jake-like pump. "Tell me why I shouldn't kill you where you stand, McVey. You came to Los Angeles a few months back, and being a cop and a turncoat, decided my sister needed some jail time to straighten her out."

McVey wove a roundabout path through a crop of evergreens. "Why would I do that after fifteen years of silence?"

"I don't know." For the moment Westor sounded uncertain. "I don't, but it doesn't matter." Anger tightened his tone. "Dicks came for her six weeks ago. She rabbited and wound up wrapping her car around a power pole. Took three and a half hours to peel the wreck away so paramedics could pull her out. In the end, they covered her with a sheet and drove her to the morgue."

McVey hadn't known that. But he'd known Westor's sister, and an alcoholic haze had been her answer to most of life's problems, big and small.

"She was all I had, McVey." Loss layered over loathing. "It's not a coincidence. You came to Los Angeles and two days later the cops had a line on my sister."

"I'm sorry she's dead, Westor, but I didn't draw that line. And I sure as hell didn't cross it."

"Well, I say you did, and I've come all the way here to say it to your face."

Lowering to a crouch, McVey sized up a tangle of brush that could hide a dozen large men. He considered drawing his gun, but when the leaves separated slightly and he spied the laser light on Westor's rifle, he opted for hand-to-hand.

"See how you feel when you lose someone who matters." Westor jerked the rifle sideways. "That tasty lady I saw you with tonight, for example."

Although his stomach clenched, McVey saw his opportunity and took it.

If Westor spotted the motion, he didn't swing around fast enough to evade it. McVey's forearm snaked across his throat, cutting off his oxygen and reducing his protest to a wet gurgle as he tried to shake his attacker off. Finally, with his eyes beginning to roll, Westor gave McVey's wrist a limp slap.

"Yeah, as if I'm gonna believe that. Kick the rifle away." McVey tightened his grip when Westor hesitated. "Do it now."

The hesitation became a gagging cough. "Okay, you win." The rifle spun off. "It's gone, and now neither of us can see a frigging thing. Tree could fall and kill us both. Still, it might be worth dying to know I'd be taking you with me."

"Always a possibility," McVey agreed. "But I think you missed your opportunity with the trees."

"Are you kid—?" In the process of tossing his head,

Westor stopped struggling and let his gaze roll skyward. "What happened to the wind?"

"It died."

"Just like that?" Westor made a scoffing sound. "Wind's not alive. It can't die as fast as a person. One of which your tasty lady is."

McVey set his mouth menacingly close to Westor's ear. "I'm only going to say this once, old friend, so you want to listen. If anything—" he cinched Westor's arm for emphasis "—I mean anything at all happens to Amara, I'll find you and I'll kill you."

Westor craned his neck for more air. "That's not fair. Way I heard it, there's a strong chance the lady has a truckload of heavy looking to squash her."

"Yeah? Who's your little bird, Westor?"

"Woman at the bar where the fight went down doesn't like your lady much. Told someone on the phone a nasty dude named Sparks could be looking to do her."

"In that case, you might want to think seriously about leaving town."

"I'll leave when I'm ready, and not before. I didn't come all this way to tip my hat at you, McVey. I want to watch you squirm, knowing I'm here, knowing I know how it used to be, how you used to live and who you stepped on to get out." His teeth gleamed in profile. "It's not as if the tasty lady's hard to look at."

With a warning squeeze, McVey released his prisoner and shoved him forward. "Did the woman in the bar happen to mention that my tasty lady's got the blood of a three-hundred-year-old witch in her veins?"

On his knees and coughing, Westor rubbed his throat. "Come on, man, you don't believe that spooked-up crap, do you?"

McVey slung the rifle over his shoulder. "I believe what

I see. Amara wanted the wind gone and, what do you know, it is. So here's the really intriguing question." His grin fell just short of evil. "What do you think would happen if she wanted you gone, too?"

Chapter Seven

Amara woke to find a raven staring at her from the ledge outside her window. Now, there was an interesting start to her first full day in Maine. On the upside, there'd been no spiders in her bed last night, and ravens, for all the local superstitions about them, had never frightened her.

McVey was another matter. She'd dreamed about him—hot, vivid dreams that had culminated with the two of them having sex in a north woods clearing filled with pointy boulders. The location might have been questionable, but the sex had been spectacular.

She replayed the highlights while she showered and dressed in a pair of faded jeans, black boots and a charcoal sweater the same color as her eyes. As far as Lieutenant Michaels's death, Willy Sparks's mission and the come-and-go man with the big knife and the creep-show leer went, she shut those thoughts away for examination later. That being after she'd poured at least two cups of coffee into her system.

The raven watched while she tidied the room but flew off with a noisy caw when she turned for the door. Very odd.

There was no sign of McVey on the second floor and no sound of him in the kitchen. At 8:15 a.m. on a misty Thursday morning, she imagined he was busy processing the handful of hungover brawlers who'd smashed up her uncle's bar last night.

Better for the brawlers that McVey should mete out the punishment than her uncle. She was chuckling at that thought as she pushed through the swinging door. Two steps in, the chuckle gave way to stunned silence.

"Uncle Lazarus." She made herself smile. "What a… nice surprise." She raised her hands, palms out. "For the record, I didn't throw a single punch at the Red Eye."

"Never crossed my mind you did, niece. Taught you to kick and jab and get your knee up whenever possible. But all punching'll get you is a fistful of swollen knuckles."

"Right." Why was she drawing a blank here? "Would you like some coffee?"

"Coffee is the devil's brew."

Strangely, his unyielding attitude relaxed her. "As I recall, you used to tell Nana I was the devil's spawn. Maybe that's why I can't start my day without caffeine."

"Likely so."

He hadn't taken his raven-black eyes off her, hadn't moved in his seat or altered his expression since she'd come in. Although his stare was designed to intimidate, she held it for five long seconds before skirting the table and reaching for the pot of coffee McVey, bless him, must have brewed earlier.

Lazarus Blume had always been a riveting man, and fifteen years had done nothing to diminish that quality. He might be a little leaner around the cheekbones, but he still made her think of a pilgrim, right down to his plain clothes, his gray-streaked beard and the hair that stuck up in windblown tufts.

Determined to find whatever humor she could in the situation, Amara brought her mug back to where he sat. "There was a raven outside my window this morning,

Uncle. He was watching me exactly the way you are now. If I didn't know better, I'd swear you were him in human form."

"And I'd say you were spouting useless Bellam rhetoric to avoid an unpleasant conversation."

"Which would be an appropriate tactic since I'm a Bellam."

He thrust himself forward. "You're a Blume as well, and don't you forget it."

"My mother—"

"Gave you the surname that was given to her by her mother. I know how the Bellam family works, Amara. I also know that three people with whom you had a courtroom affiliation in New Orleans are dead, and the man around whom the affiliation revolved likely engineered those deaths from his prison cell."

"Very likely. Unfortunately no one can prove it."

"Which is why you've come home to Raven's Hollow." He turned a thumping fist into an accusing finger when she opened her mouth. "Don't you dare say this isn't your home. Your mother grew up and married here, and you spent ten consecutive summers in this house with your grandmother. You're connected, as we all are, to the first settlers who landed on these shores with the intention of forging better lives for themselves."

He'd start reciting the Blume family history if she didn't stop him. So she sat back, let her lips curve and said simply, "I hear you got yourself arrested recently, Uncle. I believe drunk and disorderly was the charge."

He inhaled sharply through his nose. "I had my reasons."

Because it wasn't in Amara's nature to be cruel, she softened her tone. "I'm sure you did. And you of all people know I've done my share of wrong things." Because it *was* in her nature, she let mischief bubble up. "Like spy on a friend's sister's hot date. Or try to."

Lazarus gave an approving nod. "Best damn mucking out of stables I ever saw. And now you're a cosmetic surgeon."

"Reconstructive surgeon." Cupping her mug in her palms, she said, "Why did you come here today, Uncle? I know you don't like me."

"Don't like you," he bellowed, and pounded the table again. "Why, you were the only person, young or old, who ever made me laugh."

"I did? You did?" Amara frowned. "When?"

"The summer of your fourteenth year, when I punished you for sneaking out of this house. Your grandmother said you put a spell on me."

Why did the morning suddenly feel completely surreal to her? "I didn't—well, yes, I did. But I put the spell on your midnight snack, not you."

He nodded again. "Showed initiative. I appreciate that quality."

"I think it showed I had a temper, but in any case, the medical side of my brain says your stomach troubles didn't come from me."

"It was still a feisty counterstrike."

Amara sipped her coffee. "Aunt Maureen believed in the Bellam legend. She encouraged me to memorize a number of rhyming spells from a book she and Nana found in one of the attics at Bellam Manor. We—all of us—wanted Yolanda's brother, Larry, to stop sleepwalking, or at least to wear clothes when he did it. I failed miserably."

Her uncle flapped a hand. "My sister had a streak of ridiculous in her. Had an even bigger stubborn streak. She smoked herself into an early grave. Didn't want a service or even a family gathering. That's not right."

"It was for her. I know you would have preferred a funeral, Uncle, but Aunt Maureen hated sad faces."

"And naked sleepwalkers, it would seem."

Amara glanced up, but his saturnine expression remained intact.

Pushing her chair back, she started to ask if he'd seen McVey, but a beep from her iPhone signaled an incoming message.

"You immerse yourself in the technology craze, too, do you?"

His stoic expression made her grin. "Let me guess. You think technology's only a step below caffeine on the devil's list of temptations."

"Can't tell you that, as I own a similar device. But I set it to vibrate when I'm socializing face-to-face."

"It's probably one of my colleagues in New Orleans. I had to reschedule several surgeries on the drive to..." Her voice trailed off. "Jackson."

She stared unbelieving, first at her phone, then at the counter next to her. If her uncle spoke, and she thought he probably did, she only heard a freakish buzz, and even that was drowned out by the roar of blood in her ears.

She knew, vaguely knew, that the screen door slammed and someone else came into the kitchen.

McVey. Had to be.

He said something and crossed to the counter. Because she was already there, it was easy enough to catch his arm and stop him from reaching for a mug.

"Probably not the best idea," she said, showing him the message she'd just received.

DID YOU DRINK THE COFFEE, AMARA?

WILLY SPARKS SWITCHED off the stolen phone and tossed it into the trees. Time to leave, but hmm...

Uncle Jimmy was far more intrigued by small towns than he was by big cities. He claimed you could live in one your whole life, know everybody by name yet never know for sure who might be doing what to whom.

Maybe he was right. While the quite lovely Amara Bellam was inside her grandmother's edge-of-the-woods house, undoubtedly thinking she'd been poisoned—too bad about the police chief showing up, but not every circumstance could be foreseen—a truly fascinating situation was unfolding a mere fifty yards away.

Perched in the branches of a leafy chestnut tree, Willy spied someone dressed in shades of brown and green. Someone with binoculars and a large hunting rifle, who appeared to be watching the people in the house.

"I'D BE ROYALLY pissed off if I could get my heart to beat normally again." Amara checked the tips of her fingers for any discoloration. "You swear you made this coffee, McVey?"

"Made it and drank two cups before I left."

Her uncle nodded. "I've been sitting here since he left, so I can tell you no one's tampered with it. Unless the tampering was done to the beans themselves. Then you'd both be poisoned."

"More likely we'd be dead," McVey remarked.

"Could be we're all dead," her uncle postulated, "and having this conversation wherever we wound up."

McVey poured some of the brewed coffee into a jar and capped it. "That'd be hell for me."

"Me, as well," Lazarus agreed. "Since I don't drink coffee, though, I must have died some other way. Maybe my heart gave out."

Amara pressed lightly on her temples. "Excuse me, people, but am I the only one here who thinks this so-called conversation is almost as bent as the person who sent the message? Wait a second…" She narrowed accusing eyes at her uncle. "You were here before McVey left?"

"I had business," he said stiffly.

"Business with a man who arrested you and whose butt you should have but didn't put in a sling?" She aimed an I-told-you-so smile at McVey. "See? Males get preferential treatment over females."

"We were talking poison, Red." McVey opened the bag and sniffed the coffee beans, a sight that did nothing to quiet her still-jumping nerves. "We should stay on topic."

"That being someone—undoubtedly Willy Sparks— wants me to know how easy it would be for him to kill me. And a strong dose of psychological terror never hurts, either."

Her uncle stood. "What do you propose to do about this, Chief McVey?"

"What I can." McVey picked up and tapped Amara's phone. "Sparks is a pro. It'll take more than a lucky guess to identify him. No one outside the family has a description, and no one within it will talk. You talk, you suffer. I understand Jimmy has a long-standing policy in that regard."

"The Night of the Raven is coming up fast." Amara paced off her jitters. "People are already arriving for the event."

"I told my late sister's nephew he could reopen Blume House to guests for the duration." The look her uncle shot McVey had *challenge* written all over it. "What will you do about that?"

McVey glanced from the phone to her uncle and back. "I could suggest the name of the place be changed to the Hotel California and hope that that alone would cause the out-of-towners to turn tail. But more realistically, I'll run incoming names and license plates, see what comes up."

"That won't—"

"He can't arrest people for being strangers," Amara interrupted her uncle. "And he can't treat every stranger as if he or she were a criminal."

"Hit man," Lazarus corrected.

"Yes, thank you, I was trying not to use that phrase. The best idea—" she looked at McVey "—is for me to leave."

"Been down that road, Red. Even if you could slip away—unlikely in my opinion—Willy won't be happy, and neither will some of your relatives."

Because he hadn't raised his head to speak, Amara grabbed a handful of his hair and did it for him. "Fine. Give me a viable alternative."

"Joe Blume." He held up her phone. "The message you received was sent from Two Toes Joe's cell."

Amara released him because…well, mostly because his eyes and mouth were even more riveting today than they had been last night, and she really didn't need to be quite as aware of that as she suddenly was.

"So Willy Sparks is a thief as well as a murderer," her uncle said. "Is that your point?"

Amara held McVey's gaze. "I think his point is simply an expansion of what he said before. Not only is Willy Sparks here, but he's already connected some of the dots. If I leave the area, I'll still die. I just won't be the only member of my family to do it."

THEY CLIMBED UP to the attic, where the overview of the north woods tended to be impressive. Although Amara had hoped her uncle wouldn't follow them, he pushed through the trapdoor a few seconds behind her.

He wouldn't have it in him to "feel" the room, she

thought, certainly not the way she'd felt it as a child. Family history books claimed Sarah had come here to hone her craft. Whether she'd done so alone or not had never been determined. Unfortunately much of Sarah's life remained a mystery, even today.

She'd conjured things, Amara knew that much. The air smelled faintly of herbs and even the must of three centuries couldn't erase lingering traces of woodsmoke.

She ran her fingers over a stack of dusty trunks. "Antiques hunters would see this place as a treasure trove."

McVey pushed aside an enormous cobweb on his way to the cupola. "Spiders, mice and birds sure as hell do."

"Spiders, right. Forgot about those." Amara twitched away a shiver. "I was phobic as a kid." She nodded. "Ladder's there, McVey. I'm not sure how much better the view will be, though. And unless he's a complete fool, Willy Sparks won't be hanging around. Why are we doing this?"

"Because I saw a flash downstairs. Possibly light bouncing off glass or metal."

"Great. So Willy Sparks is a fool and he's abandoned the subtle approach."

"Or he has backup."

"An even more cheerful thought."

"It's also possible a raven picked up a piece of glass or metal and dropped it in a tree."

"Whatever the source, I can't just hang around and wait for a hit man to do his job."

"We'll have to believe that McVey will do his job first." Her uncle spoke from the top rung of the ladder stairs. "Meanwhile, Amara, you have excellent medical skills."

She knew what was coming. However, a spider the size of a baby rat crawled out from behind an old chair and caused her muscles to seize. "You want me to help Dr. Whoever at— There's a clinic in the Hollow, right?"

"There's a midwife," he said.

"And for anyone who's not pregnant?"

"There's the Cove."

"Which has?"

McVey hopped from the cupola. "Sorry to say, the best we can boast is a nearsighted former army medic who still hasn't grasped the concept of painkillers. Fog's rolling in. If someone's out there, he won't be able to see us."

Amara leaned over to check on the tarantula-size spider's progress. "What aren't you telling us, McVey?"

"You can't read my mind?"

"Be a terrifying prospect if she could." Her uncle glanced down, pulled a BlackBerry from his pocket and scowled at the screen. "I hate goat's milk," he declared.

"Must be Seth," Amara said while her uncle raised the phone to his ear. "What?" she asked when McVey grinned. Then she got it and blew out a breath. "His nephew, Seth Blume, has a farm in the middle of nowhere, two hundred miles north of the Cove. He raises chickens, pigs and goats, McVey. I don't read minds."

He started toward her. "But you do other things."

"I'm told I bake a mean lasagna."

It occurred to her when she stopped scanning for spiders that she'd let him get too close. Before she could sidestep, he wrapped his fingers around the nape of her neck.

"Look at me, Amara."

"It would be hard not to from here."

"What do you see?"

A mouth she was tempted to kiss. But he didn't mean that, so she shifted her gaze to where he wanted it—the cheek she'd scratched last night.

"They weren't gouges. Don't give me more credit than I deserve."

"They're gone."

"I still see marks."

"Yeah?" He lowered his head and, damn it, made her breath stutter. "What would Jake's kid brother see?"

"The same thing as anyone with a brain the size of a snow pea." She refused to break eye contact. "I'm hoping yours is bigger than that."

McVey's lips crooked into a smile. She thought for a moment he was going to kiss her, but her uncle cleared his throat and the moment vanished.

"Seth can't get hold of his mother."

Dragging her eyes from McVey's, Amara searched her mind for a name. Hannah, she thought.

"His mother's your cousin, isn't she, Uncle? People used to call her, uh, your cousin. Does Seth think something's wrong?"

"A squirrel bit her two weeks back. She phoned him last Sunday to say her leg had swelled up like a balloon. Seth's been trying to contact her for three days. He wants me to make sure she's all right, maybe take her some aspirin."

"Because a person with an infected leg must have a headache to go with it. Where does she live?"

He aimed a look up Bellam Mountain. "She moved to the manor six months ago. She wanted solitude. The outer wings are only partly habitable since Molly and Sadie Bellam left. Road that takes you there's bumpier than the stairway to hell."

"Heaven," Amara corrected absently.

McVey gave the yard below a final visual sweep. "I drove up to Bellam Manor last fall, Red. Nothing about that road can be called heavenly."

"Making it a perfect counterpoint to the state of my life." Without looking over, she indicated the dense fog that was beginning to obliterate the upper limbs of the trees. "Coming from the north, right?"

"Yep."

"That's the way to Bellam Manor."

"Know it. You might want to pack a few things. We can pick up any medical supplies you think you'll need in the Hollow. I'll make sure both towns are covered deputy-wise."

Amara brought her eyes calmly to his. "I could tell you I know the way and you don't have to come."

"You could," McVey agreed. "But then I'd have to tell you I went through the kitchen cupboards after you got that text message. There were two bags of coffee inside. I picked up supplies yesterday. I only bought one."

Chapter Eight

"Take whatever you need, Dr. Bellam." The pharmacist poked his Buddy Holly glasses up a little higher. "Just fill out the supply form so I know what to restock." He ticked a finger behind him and whispered, "Bathroom. Gotta go."

Amara selected the antibiotics and anti-inflammatories she required. She added a bottle of hydrogen peroxide, another of rubbing alcohol, a roll of gauze and two candy bars, then hoisted the substantially heavier medical bag onto her left shoulder.

The one and only pharmacy in Raven's Hollow had been retrofitted into the back of an old-fashioned general store. The shelves were high and crowded, every floor plank squeaked and, when running at full capacity, the ancient refrigeration units tended to shimmy away from the walls. A quarter of the lights were either burned out or flickering, and she imagined the thirty-year-old cash register probably still died in the middle of a lengthy transaction.

Some things never changed.

"Excuse me." A woman with huge brown eyes and a noticeable overbite waved a hand. "Do you have this lipstick in other colors? I'm looking for bubble-gum pink. It's my trademark shade."

"Yours and my cousin Yolanda's. I don't work here." Amara lowered her bag to the floor. "The cashier's at lunch and the pharmacist's in the back. I just came in to shop-lift some drugs."

"Cool—and bold. I'm Mina Shell. I'm in town for the… Oh, there, I see one." She reached over the glass counter to snag a tube. "Blast O' Pink. Perfect. D'you suppose I could leave the money with a note? Except I haven't got any paper. Or a pen."

Amara was tearing a blank sheet from the supply pad when she heard a creak behind her. Before she could raise her head, a man gripped her wrist and jerked her around.

"Hey, there, gorgeous. I've been looking for you all over this freaky bird town." He caught the other woman by the scruff of her neck and squeezed. "Not so fast, Pretty in Pink. I got a few things I want to say to Glinda while we're more or less alone."

The knife Amara had glimpsed the previous night dangled over her shoulder. The man rubbed a thumb across the blade and offered a lewd smile. "Don't you just love how some store owners are so trusting? Not a security camera in sight—if you're wishing and hoping, that is. Okay, so, brass tacks time, Glin." He leaned in closer. "Is this your real body or do you fog a man's mind so he only thinks you're a babe? Shut up," he snapped when Mina squealed.

"You're pinching me."

"Duh, yeah. In case you haven't guessed, I'm not a nice guy. And speaking of not nice—" he turned to Amara "—I think it's time you and me—"

It was as far as he got. Amara brought her heel down on his instep, plowed an elbow into his ribs and, spinning free, took a swing at his head with the bottle of rubbing alcohol she'd managed to slip from her medical bag.

She hadn't expected to knock him out, but she had hoped to stun him. Instead he whipped the knife up and showed his teeth.

"I am so gonna do you," he growled.

Spotting a movement at the rear of the store, Amara shouted, "Benny, get McVey." She straight-armed the plastic alcohol bottle as if it would shield her from a knife the size of a machete.

Thankfully the man glanced over, saw the pharmacist and, shoving Mina aside, took off through the side exit.

Lowering the bottle, Amara released her fear on a trembling breath. Pale-cheeked and clutching his phone, the pharmacist rushed forward.

"Are you hurt? Did he hurt you? I called the police station. I'm so sorry."

"I broke a heel," Mina told Amara. "And a fingernail." She blinked. "All I wanted was a tube of lipstick and I got pinched, shoved and maybe almost decapitated by the Machete Kid. Not sure I should hang for the Raven thing after all. I mean, that was one humongous knife."

It was also the second time Amara had seen it.

She was returning the rubbing alcohol to her medical bag when Jake burst through the front door, armed and clearly prepared for battle.

"Where's the creep?" he demanded, waving his .38 Special back and forth.

Amara eased the barrel aside with her index finger. "He left by the exit to the alley."

Jake's jaw clenched. "You let him go? Why didn't you…?"

"Hemorrhoids," she reminded him. Then she shrugged. "As long as you insist on believing in the absurd."

"I saw the knife." Mina piped up. "But I was too scared to notice the guy's face. Sorry."

"I saw his face." The pharmacist poked at his glasses. "Saw it here a few minutes ago and through my bedroom window early this morning. The man wearing it came out of the building across the alley, the one with the raven and the witch on the door that kids keep spray painting red. You know the place, Deputy. It's where Yolanda Bellam lives."

PANDEMONIUM REIGNED AT the station house. No fewer than ten voices shouted at the same time. McVey made no attempt to separate one from the other. Instead he tried to keep an eye on Amara, who stood in front of the dispatcher's desk, relating her account of the incident to one of the Harden twins.

"Stop badgering me." Yolanda's shrill whine rose above the din. "Is it my fault some jerk with a knife happened to be sneaking out of a building that has three other apartments in it besides mine at whatever o'clock in the morning? McVey…"

"I said take her statement, Jake, not accuse her of harboring a fugitive."

"He wasn't a fugitive when she harbored him."

"I didn't harbor him." Stepping directly into McVey's line of vision, Yolanda walked the fingers of both hands up his shirt. "My brother wasn't there when I got up this morning, so I can't prove I was alone. Jake thinks I'm lying, but you believe me, don't you?"

What he believed, he thought as he eased her aside, was that he should turn in his badge, hunt Westor Hall down and hang him from one of the tortured oaks by his—

"I hate to interrupt a man who looks as if he wants to put a bullet in someone's head." Amara tapped his arm from the side. "But is there any chance of us ditching this town before the fog that's rolling out to sea gives way to the nasty black clouds that are creeping down from the north? Because the only thing worse than the road to Bellam Manor in a downpour is—well, actually, short of a mudslide, not a whole lot."

McVey indicated the crowd. "How many of these people were in the pharmacy when Wes—the guy with the knife appeared?"

She regarded him for a moment before perusing the room. "The pharmacist and Mina, but she freaked and left when Jake started waving a second gun around."

"Smart woman."

"Benny's your best witness, McVey. And maybe one or two people from the alley. Everyone else is either bored and curious or waiting for the Red Eye to open."

McVey reached around her to intercept Yolanda's curled fingers. "No scratching," he warned.

She glared at Amara. "You stayed at Nana's last night."

Amara glared right back. "Pretty sure you said I couldn't say with you."

"I also said…" She glanced at McVey, then back. "I hate you."

"So no change there."

When Yolanda's hands balled at her sides, McVey got between them. "Lazarus had a call from his nephew, Seth, this morning, Yolanda. He thinks his mother might need medical attention."

She sniffed. "Since when does Seth worry about his mother? If it doesn't cluck or have four legs, he doesn't notice or care about it. That includes Hannah—who's a story unto herself—and why Lazarus gives two hoots about her is beyond me."

Pushing a hefty man aside, Jake joined them. "Seth's only worried his mother'll kick off before Lazarus does. Then, poof, there'll go his chance of worming any inheritance money he might be in line to receive from her." He shrugged an irritable shoulder. "Lazarus can't stand Seth. Or me. Or my brother. Or half the Blumes, or any of the Bellams in either town."

"He likes Nana," Amara pointed out. "He also holds the title on Bellam Manor."

Jake's lips peeled away from his teeth. "Well, hell, Amara, anyone could get past the Bellam name to own a house and land that are worth a fortune. As for actual Bellams, you can't blame the guy for not liking them. The only one I ever dated threatened to turn me into a toad."

McVey pressed on his now-throbbing eyes. "Only threatened?" he asked. "Do your job, Jake. Talk to Benny and anyone who saw anything in the alley. Send the rest of these people home."

Jake's jaw tightened, but he nodded. "What about the guy with the knife? Are we just gonna let him roam around free until whenever?"

"He won't be roaming, Deputy."

"He will if we don't go after him."

"He doesn't need to roam, Jake." Amara glanced toward the north woods. "All he needs to do is follow McVey and me up the mountain to Bellam Manor."

IF WESTOR WAS SANE—and McVey figured he had his moments—he wouldn't attempt to follow them even partway up the mountain.

By 4:00 p.m., the sky had turned an ominous shade of black. Swollen clouds tinged with purple collided and swirled. Where they did, tiny bolts of electricity shot from one to the other.

"This is fascinating, really." Amara secured her medical bag in the space behind her seat. "The family history books claim that Hezekiah Blume became a raven on a night that started exactly like this."

McVey shoved their backpacks in from the driver's side. "He did."

"Did what?"

"Become a raven during an electrical storm.... And how the hell would I know that?"

"Maybe you're possessed. Don't crush the candy bars, McVey. We'll need the sugar buzz by the time we reach the manor."

"We'll need more than a sugar buzz, and I've got a bottle of it safely stowed." Disinclined to pursue his earlier remark, he climbed in and motioned for Amara to buckle up. "Believe me when I tell you the potholes on the Hollow Road can swallow a large truck if you hit them straight on."

She pulled the shoulder harness across. "You're just full of optimism today, aren't you?"

"My goal is to get us up the mountain and back in one piece."

"I applaud the sentiment, McVey, but I have to tell you, too much secrecy makes me twitchy."

He felt her eyes on his face.

"You know the guy with the Texas-size knife, don't you? Know him personally, I mean."

He could lie, but why bother? So he forced his muscles to relax and draped a hand over the steering wheel. "You're observant, Red, I'll give you that. Jake hasn't figured it out yet."

"Jake wasn't with us last night when you made your one-man foray into the woods. We both know that rifles are more powerful than handguns, and I'm betting the one we heard came equipped with an infrared scope. If the shooter wanted you dead, we'd be digging your grave right now."

Answer or evade? McVey opted for middle ground with a leading edge of truth.

"I recognized the shot pattern, Amara. Three times three. It's a signal we used to use. It also had the benefit of making enough noise that anyone in the vicinity who shouldn't be there got the hell out fast."

"Where exactly were they getting the hell out of?"

"A potentially dangerous situation."

"That's not an answer."

"Yes, it is. Or it's as much of one as I'm going to give you right now. Let's leave it at…I wasn't always a cop, and even after I became one, not every cop I met lived by the same code."

He felt more than saw her exasperation.

"Are you ever not cryptic—" She broke off to swing around in her seat. "I saw a light. Did you see a light?"

"Three streaking overhead and a more substantial one behind us. The one behind could be a local heading for the north woods. I'm told there are a number of pocket communities scattered around. I've also heard about, but haven't crossed paths with yet, a group of nomads who live off the grid in a collection of campers, trailers and caravans."

"The raven tamers." She strained to see farther back. "Mostly Blumes. They teach ravens to do tricks and create mechanical ones that can do what the real ravens won't. The tamers are bound to come into the Hollow for the Night. They'll put on shows, sell their amazing raven crafts, then disappear back into the woods with tons of orders for what they do best."

"Which is?"

"Brewing and bottling raven's blood—wine, not actual blood—and their signature 'gonna knock you out for two whole days if you're not extremely careful' whiskey."

He knew he shouldn't be amused, but his lips quirked even so. "Why haven't I heard about these people?"

Her grin was a punch of lust straight to his groin. "You're joking, right—Police Chief McVey?"

"Amara, in the past fourteen months, I've unearthed half a dozen stills. Unless I see some kind of trouble directly related to one of them, I'm willing to turn a blind eye."

"Ty isn't."

"I'm not Ty."

"I got that right off, but gaining the raven tamers' trust will take a bit longer."

"Have you met any of them?"

"Only Brigham, and only because I bumped into him on the single occasion I visited Bellam Manor. It was a family thing. A funeral. A really old Bellam uncle wanted to be buried in the really old cemetery behind the house. It was the spookiest experience I've ever…" She pivoted in her seat. "I saw another beam. I'm sure it was a headlight."

He nodded, glanced in the mirror. The road, such as it was, had already become a serpentine river of rain and mud. And, as he recalled, there was worse to come.

Thunder began to rumble overhead as the grade increased. Amara kept her gaze fixed behind them. "Do you think it's the knife guy or Willy Sparks?"

"I'd go with Willy."

"I knew you'd say that." She craned her neck for a better view. "So when was the last time you had a report on the bridge? Obviously it was passable when Sadie and Molly lived at the manor, but it's been a few years since Sadie got married and moved to New York and Molly left to live with Ty."

McVey ground his teeth as his left rear tire slammed through a pothole. "Road's a lot worse than it was last fall. As for the bridge, we'll see when we get there."

If they got there. An extended peal of thunder shuddered through the mountainside and up into his truck. The only positive he could see here was that whoever was behind them would need to navigate the same minefield to reach the manor.

Assuming the goal was to reach the manor and not run them over the edge.

"You're looking in that rearview mirror entirely too much, McVey. Do you think he's going to ram your truck?"

"Odds are. This road's got *death trap* written all over it. We shoot off and go for a roll, there'll be no way to prove it was a deliberate act." He glanced at her, his expression mildly humorous. "Wishing you'd said no to your uncle yet?"

More tiny lightning bolts zapped from cloud to cloud. "Maybe. A little. But the truth is, Hannah's ten years up on Uncle Lazarus, and he's old. She used to babysit him when he was a kid."

"Lazarus was a kid? Not sure I can picture that."

"I'll admit it's a stretch imagination-wise. Jake told me people in both towns call her Mother Goose." Amara held up both hands. "Hey, I never met the woman. I'm only repeating." She grabbed the dash when McVey swerved around a jagged cluster of ruts. "Whatever she's called, I think it's time for her to swap the seclusion of Bellam Manor for a more accessible north woods' cabin."

McVey swore as a thin beam of light streaked across the rear windshield at the precise moment the rain, already pounding down, became a veritable waterfall. Where was the damn bridge?

"Half a mile ahead." Amara sent him a quick smile. "Read it in your face, Chief. I don't think he's gaining on us."

"He's not."

"So you see—" She broke off to stare. "My God, those dips in the road look like duck ponds."

"Hang on" was all McVey said.

It took him fifteen long minutes to maneuver through the damaged sections. A dozen potholes and three hairpin turns later, he spotted the bridge.

Amara studied the sagging structure. "I don't see getting across any other way except on foot, do you?"

He reached for his gun on the dash. "On foot and preferably naked. Clothes have weight," he added, then grinned. "Plus the visual gave me a wicked sexual rush."

"I'm flattered, but I'd prefer an assessment from the part of your brain that lives above the waist."

"The bridge is crap, Red. We'll need our rain gear." He opened the glove box. "Can you hit a moving target?"

"If we're lucky, we'll never find out."

Unfortunately, judging by the next slash of light, their pursuer was less than half a mile behind them.

Because he'd dealt with hysteria before, McVey set his hands on her shoulders and checked her eyes. They were dark, determined and striking enough that his train of thought almost slipped away. Did slip away for a moment. And he knew he wouldn't be getting it back in a hurry when the corners of her mouth curved into a teasing smile.

"On the subject of wicked sexual rushes…" she began.

Lightning forked overhead. As it did, her eyes sparkled silver. A second later McVey's hand was in her hair and his mouth was on hers. And somewhere on the hazy fringes of his mind, it occurred to him that the danger in his truck might be much greater than the danger behind them.

Chapter Nine

The taste of him plunged Amara's senses into a whirlpool of desire. A thousand electric volts sparked in her head. She wanted to touch every inch of him with her mouth and with her hands.

She felt his fingers on her face and heard the moan that emerged from her throat. While his tongue explored, she ran her palms over his chest and absorbed the feel of him. Sleek, hard muscles; smooth, firm skin…and heat everywhere she touched.

She nipped his lower lip, bit the corners of his mouth, then moved to the button of his jeans and prepared to enjoy herself.

Miniature lightning bolts snapped the air like whips. Two of them seemed to race along her arms while a third sizzled down her spine. She wished she could block reality and go back to savoring, but something shifted in her brain and she pulled back. She needed to breathe quite badly, needed to think even more.

"McVey, we can't… This is crazy. We're crazy." She struggled to reorient and settle herself. "There's a homicidal nutball on the road behind us and we're playing Spin the Bottle in your truck."

"More like Russian roulette." He kissed her again and made her head swim, before pulling away to stare straight into her eyes. "Okay, here's the deal. You go first. Carefully. We hear shots, you hit the ground. Got it?"

"Shots, ground, got it."

Lunacy, she thought as they tugged on rain gear and loaded up with packs. What rational woman let herself be sidetracked by the prospect of sex—okay, potentially amazing sex—when she knew there was someone who probably wanted her dead close behind?

Since the question had no answer and a premature darkness had begun to steal across the mountain, she let it go. For now.

Bellam Bridge was a blend of deteriorating wood planks and badly rusted iron framework. With regular maintenance, it might have lasted another two decades. Without it, Amara's body weight appeared to tax the entire support system.

McVey followed her onto the shrieking planks, close enough to grab her but with a wide enough gap between them that they were never on the same piece of wood at the same time.

Amara inched forward and told herself that any sponginess she felt was her imagination working overtime. Neither of them was going to plunge to death on the rocks below.

Razor-thin shafts of lightning continued to electrify the sky. If there was another form of light behind them, she could no longer see it.

One step, two, three... Every muscle in her body threatened to seize. She took another step, heard a loud crack and willed the nightmare to end. How long was this stupid bridge anyway?

Her nerves had long since passed the breaking point when she spotted solid ground. Put her foot on solid ground. Considered dropping to her knees and kissing that ground.

Instead she released a shivery breath and shouted, "The manor's a mile away by road, but there's a stone path—really steep—or there used to be, that can get us there much faster."

"Go for it," he shouted back and gave her a nudge. "Eyes forward," he said when she turned to peer past his arm. "I saw headlights behind my truck a few seconds ago."

Being a doctor had definite moments of sucking, Amara reflected.

She was able to locate the old path without the aid of a flashlight. In another ten minutes, however, they'd be relying entirely on the storm and whatever other light sources McVey had thought to bring along.

In areas where the stone steps had crumbled, she was forced to claw her way up. In others, McVey gripped her waist and gave her a boost.

It felt as if they climbed for hours, but it was probably only twenty minutes. Did a thin beam of light bob directly behind them? Did she care when breathing had become an exercise in pain, her knees and elbows were bruised and her palms had been scraped raw?

Drawing on the last of her strength, Amara hauled herself up and over the edge.

Bellam Manor stood like a brooding black fortress against the stormy sky. Rain blurred the peaks and towers, but as she recalled, even on a good day, nothing about the place said welcome.

"The central core of the house splits the wings where my cousins used to live," she shouted when McVey pulled himself up beside her. "We could search all night and not find Hannah. So…" Lowering her pack, she unzipped the top flap and removed her iPhone. "Uncle Lazarus gave me her number. For some weird and wonderful reason, wireless tech works up here."

"Put it down to residual Bellam magic and the fortunate placement of a cell tower." McVey crouched near the edge of the precipice and looked down. "If you get through, tell her to leave the house dark."

Booming thunder caused the rocks under Amara's feet to vibrate. She tried Hannah's number three times with no luck.

"Guess we'll have to search after all." Slipping the phone into her pocket, she peered over McVey's shoulder. "Any sign of pursuit?"

"Not so far."

"That's good, right?"

"Not necessarily."

She sighed. "You'd think I'd learn not to ask." Turning, she regarded the manor. "East or west wing?"

"Anything coming to you?"

"Other than a strong desire to run, no." But she turned her mind as well as her eyes to the house, because…well, why not?

Sensing nothing, she pointed at the ruined central core.

A giant raven's-head knocker on the double front doors echoed louder than the storm. Now, there was an inviting sound, Amara reflected, and twisted the brass entry ring. The right door swung inward on eerily silent hinges.

"How is it possible that hinges not creaking is a thousand times creepier than the other way around?" She set her pack on a floor littered with plaster, glass, dust and wood. "Hannah?"

McVey produced two powerful flashlights and shone his up the once-grand staircase to the remnants of a cobwebbed chandelier.

"It's shaped like a pentagram." Pulling out her phone, Amara tried Hannah's number again. "Do you hear a ring?"

"Are you serious?"

But they listened for several seconds.

After turning a circle in place, Amara ended the call and shook her head. "She's not here, McVey."

He crossed to a narrow window. "Pick a wing, then, Red."

"At the risk of sounding like Sarah, I don't think she's anywhere in the house. No vibes," she added when he glanced at her.

McVey returned to his scan of the ceiling. "That probably shouldn't make me feel better, but it does. She might be in one of the outbuildings. Or the cave."

"There's a cave?"

"In the woods behind the manor."

Exasperation mixed with uncertainty. "You're not on some kind of medication I should know about, are you, McVey? Who told you—?"

With so many dense shadows enfolding them, she didn't see him move, didn't realize he was behind her until his hand covered her mouth and his lips moved against her ear.

"Your uncle told me about it. There's someone outside. He's circling the manor."

Amara's heart shot into her throat. Unable to speak around it, she let him slip his backup gun between her fingers.

Jimmy Sparks's face darted through her head. Teeth gleamed, and Jimmy morphed into the man with the big knife. Not Willy Sparks, her blipping mind recalled. Not if McVey was to be believed.

A little unsure, she flattened herself against the wall while he watched through the window.

"Whoever it is moves quickly and well," he remarked.

"I imagine most assassins would."

"He's heading for the west wing." McVey pushed an extra ammo clip into her free hand. "Don't shoot unless you're certain of your target."

"No, wait, McVey, you can't…"

But he could and did. And left her wishing she really had inherited some of Sarah's power, enough at least to put a binding spell on him.

Lowering to her knees, she braced her wrists on the sill and ordered herself to listen for sounds within the storm.

She spied an arc of light to her right. It slashed across the clearing and for less than a heartbeat of time revealed a figure dressed in shiny black. The person was bent low and appeared to be running away from the manor.

Amara eased up for a clearer look. But the lightning winked out, the person vanished and only the thunder and pelting rain remained.

Two seconds later a gunshot exploded outside.

THE BULLET WAS a rogue, McVey suspected. And it came from a handgun, not a rifle, which tended to be Westor's weapon of choice. So…probably not him.

Lightning raced through the sky in long, skinny bolts. McVey moved between flashes and kept an eye peeled for any motion that didn't involve rain, flying objects or swaying trees.

Fifty feet ahead, a leg disappeared around the west side of the manor. Fixing his mind on the spot and keeping to the shadows as much as possible, he ran.

They'd called it foot pursuit back at the academy. Bad guys bolted; cops gave chase. Sometimes the bad guys got cornered and attacked, but in vast, open areas they didn't tend to launch themselves out of the darkness like human projectiles, roaring and, in the case of this particular projectile, packing upward of two hundred and fifty hairy pounds.

McVey glimpsed the human mass, but not quickly enough to avoid it. The best he could do was duck low to prevent an all-out tackle that would have landed him on a jagged clump of rocks.

As it was, the blow knocked him sideways and slammed his shoulder into the stump of a tree.

Aware that he'd only half struck his target, the man went from his knees to a feral crouch to another roaring attack in a New York second.

Knowing he'd only get one shot, McVey rolled onto his back, double-handed his Glock and, as the man rushed toward him, squeezed off two shots.

It might have been his attacker falling or a particularly violent clap of thunder, but the ground beneath McVey's feet shook. Cursing, the man swung onto his side and would have reared up if McVey hadn't used his gun to slam him in the jaw.

His attacker went down like a felled tree.

Winded, and with his shoulder throbbing, McVey took aim at a bearded face. "Give me a name, pal, and hope like hell it's one I want to hear. Because right now I'm just pissed off enough to forget I took an oath to serve and protect."

A flashlight beam sliced through the murk. As it did, he heard Amara shout, "Don't shoot him, McVey. He's not Willy Sparks. His name's Brigham Blume. He's a raven tamer."

"OUCH, AMARA."

The oversize tamer jerked, but Amara merely went with the motion and finished pumping the contents of her syringe into his tattooed upper arm.

"Both bullets penetrated flesh, Brigham. A few stitches and you'll be good to go."

"Figuratively speaking," McVey put in.

He poured three glasses of whiskey in a kitchen too tidy to have been abandoned for any length of time. When he added in the fact that the place had power—fading in and out, but working for the moment—it appeared they'd found Hannah's home. As for Hannah herself, he'd searched the entire west wing from top to bottom without success.

Brigham picked up one of the drinks, downed it and glared. "Why'd you shoot me?"

McVey tossed his own whiskey back. "Why did you attack me?"

"I thought you were the other guy. Same time I realized you weren't, I saw you had a gun. I figured if you were anything like your dumb-ass deputy, you'd be inclined to shoot first and congratulate yourself on the result."

Okay, that was a lot of information. McVey homed in on the significant point. "What other guy?"

"The one who followed you up the mountain. I noticed he was on your tail after I got on his."

"Where was that?" Amara asked.

"While you were lollygagging across the bridge. I came to collect storm noises. Around the bridge gives a great echo."

"For their amazing animated ravens," Amara informed McVey. "Nana says the raven tamers do a killer show throughout the festival, complete with sound effects."

"Other guy," McVey reminded her.

Brigham slid his glass forward for a refill. "That's all I've got, McVey. Guy followed you, I spotted him. I went up the stone path behind him, behind you. I lost him at the top, but decided to skulk a bit, because even though I shouldn't, I liked Amara when I met her all those years

back, and while you might think we live like our ancestors in the north woods, we stay connected to some of our
relatives in the Cove. We know what's what. Don't always
like to admit we know, but we do." He shrugged his good
shoulder. "I put knowing and seeing together and came
up with someone who wants Amara here to be joining her
fellow witnesses in death."

"Fellow witnesses and the cop who helped her get out
of New Orleans." McVey sent the whiskey bottle sliding
across the table.

"Soda pop's got more of a kick than this stuff," Brigham
scoffed. He jerked again. "I said, ouch, Amara."

"Heard you the first time." She pulled a suture through
his flesh and made McVey's stomach roll. "We should
check the house as well as the outbuildings for Hannah.
I might not be feeling her vibe, but my Bellam senses are
far from infallible."

"I'll help." Brigham poured himself a full six ounces of
whiskey and knocked it back as if it really was soda pop.
"Hannah's kin of a sort. Weird, but kin."

"Pot, kettle," McVey said into his glass. "How much
longer, Red?"

"All done." She tapped Brigham's shoulder. "No pulling, no fiddling. They'll dissolve as you heal. I'll give you
something for the pain."

Brigham gave McVey a hard look. "I've got that covered at home—I hope."

McVey just smiled. "Let's find Hannah."

As Amara washed her hands, she nodded at the full
second sink. "Wherever she went, Hannah left a week's
worth of dirty dishes behind."

Joining her, McVey counted ten plates, six bowls with
food hardened on the bottom and a single coffee-stained
mug that smelled like bio-diesel fuel.

He held the mug out to Brigham, who was shrugging cautiously into his jacket. "Residue of your kick-ass whiskey?"

The big man sniffed the mug. "Well, damn me. And we've been making do with ginger ale. I should've checked out the cupboards when we came in. My mind must've gone south from the pain of having two bullets drilled into my shoulder."

"You want to launch an official complaint, I'll be happy to take your statement while you're showing me around your raven tamer property." McVey picked up a wineglass that was coated red inside. "Raven's blood, I assume?"

Amara took the glass and smiled. "Nana says it's an acquired taste." She rubbed her thumb over a pink smudge on the rim. "If Hannah drank raven's blood and chased it with raven tamer whiskey, it's possible she's passed out somewhere between here and one of the outbuildings. Passed out equals no vibes. Or so the theory goes."

As a fresh round of wind and rain buffeted the manor, McVey rezipped his jacket. "Let's get this done. If Hannah's on the property, we need to find her." He regarded Brigham, who was currently rooting through the pantry. "Do you know if there's power in the other wing?"

"Doubt it." He sent Amara an evil grin. "But I'm willing to bet there're plenty of really big spiders."

BRIGHAM WAS RIGHT about the lack of power. Unfortunately he was also right about the spiders. Amara found evidence of several in each of the rooms she inspected.

"How is it possible," she asked the big raven tamer when he passed her in a dusty second-floor corridor, "that you know so specifically what terrifies me?"

"Could be a little raven told me." But he chuckled when she beamed her light directly into his face. "Okay, McVey told me. He made a sweep while you were digging out your instruments of torture. He made me look under the table. Me, Amara, the guy with two bullet holes in his arm."

"Any time you want to swear out that complaint, Blume." McVey came down the ladder stairs from the attic. "Any luck?"

Amara jerked her hand away from a sticky web. "No. You?"

"I spotted a bunch of small sheds and a larger building that was probably a barn or stable at one time."

"She might have gone to a neighbor's place," Brigham said. "How bad was her leg?"

"Swollen like a balloon according to Uncle Lazarus." Amara fastened her rain jacket and pulled on the Dodgers cap McVey had loaned her.

"You and me, left. Him, right." McVey took her hand and tossed one of the flashlights to Brigham. "Don't assume the person you saw earlier is gone."

"Because he's probably not as considerate as you and won't settle for shooting me in the shoulder."

Amara watched him slog away. "I like Brigham better, but he reminds me of Jake. Which makes sense, I suppose, since they're both Blumes, and he seems to know about your dumb-ass deputy's penchant for firearms."

McVey gave the bill of her cap a tug. "You have a strange group of relatives, Red. Barn's about two hundred feet west. Tuck in close behind me."

The wind had picked up and the rain was falling in buckets now. Mud sucked at Amara's boots and made running impossible. Even if they found Hannah, she couldn't see them getting her back to McVey's truck.

And if they couldn't get back, she thought as they approached the barn, neither could the person who'd apparently followed them. All in all, not a positive prospect for the next several hours.

The barn turned out to be even more derelict than the manor. A full third of the roof and most of the wall that faced the ocean had been torn away. There was no sign of Hannah, only a dozen or so rusty vehicles from another era.

"What now?" Amara asked when they rejoined Brigham in the central core.

McVey shone his flashlight up the staircase again. "Only place we haven't looked is here."

"Not infallible," she reminded him. "Up or down?"

"With a leg like a balloon, I doubt she'd have gone either way. This floor's our best bet."

Brigham took the front of the house, leaving the back to her and McVey.

"Oh, wow, now here's a kitchen only my great-great-many-times-grandmother would recognize." Stepping carefully, Amara beamed her light into a hearth large enough to roast an ox. She ran it over broken counters, cupboards with no doors and appliances so old their purpose eluded her. "Hannah?" Her voice echoed up to the rafters. "Brigham could be right, McVey. She might have made her way to a neighbor's—"

The last word never emerged as McVey gripped her arms and yanked her down below the level of the windowsill.

"Someone's heading into the trees."

A glimmer of lightning revealed a figure, but it could have been a deer for all Amara saw of it. Moving ahead of her, McVey led the way along the line of windows to the door.

"It's as if we crossed Bellam Bridge and stepped into

the worst horror film ever," she whispered. "What if it's another raven tamer, McVey?"

"I'll try not to shoot any vital parts. Stay here, Amara, and be ready. Anyone you don't recognize appears, fire a warning. If he keeps coming, shoot him."

He stood as he spoke and eased the door open.

Amara set a hand on the floor. She would have gone from a crouch to her knees if her fingers hadn't recognized the thing beneath them and gone still where they lay.

"McVey?" Even being a doctor, she didn't want to lower her eyes. "I, uh…could you shine your flashlight this way for a minute?"

"Not now, Red."

"Yes, now." Her throat tightened, threatened to close. Before it did, she made herself look.

McVey angled his light down. The beam bounced off a pair of green eyes. Lifeless eyes, Amara's shocked mind corrected. The lifeless green eyes of her uncle's cousin, Hannah Blume.

Chapter Ten

In Amara's opinion, Hannah had been dead for at least two days. If appearances could be believed, she'd struck her head on one of the broken counters. But given her severely swollen leg, why she'd been in this part of the house was anyone's guess.

"Maybe she was delirious." Brigham watched as McVey gathered what evidence he could without disturbing Hannah's body. "Could've wandered over here not meaning to."

"It's possible" was all McVey said, and he did so absently while taking pictures with his iPhone.

When he was finished, Brigham got a sheet from Hannah's living quarters and Amara draped it over her. Because he'd known her best, she asked Brigham to say a few words.

After a last look around the property, McVey secured the manor and they headed back to Hannah's wing.

"Power's out," he noted halfway across the yard. "All the lights on the lower floor were burning when we left."

"I didn't see a generator in any of the sheds," Brigham shouted forward.

"There was nothing in the barn, either," Amara called back.

Leaning into the house, McVey tried the light switches. When nothing happened, he flipped his jacket collar up and came back out. "With our mystery man still at large, this could turn into a hell of a long night."

"We've got gens." Brigham's surly tone told Amara quite clearly that he didn't want to take them anywhere near the raven tamers' camp. "I'll need some assurances first, though, McVey."

"Only assurance you're getting is that I'm not Ty."

Brigham's teeth appeared, but not in the form of a smile. "Makes two of us. Grab your gear and let's roll. Camp's a fair hike away."

They walked single file with Amara in the middle. Lightning continued to flicker. Thunder rumbled behind it and the rain just kept on falling.

Amara knew she should be worried about Willy Sparks, but all she could think about was Hannah's vacuous expression, her glassy eyes and, of course, the dried blood.

Whether he'd let it show or not, Uncle Lazarus would be upset. She was upset, and she hadn't known the woman.

The north woods went on forever. Although she worked out five days a week at a New Orleans fitness center, negotiating rocky paths that climbed, dipped, tilted and often vanished altogether made Amara's legs feel like rubber bands. Wherever they were going, she figured they would have crossed at least one state border before they arrived.

Gradually a sprinkling of lights came into view. As they descended into an odd-shaped clearing, trailers of various sizes, ages and states of disrepair took shape. If any permanent structures existed, Amara couldn't see them. Prepared for the worst, and with McVey close behind her, she trailed Brigham to an outlying RV.

"Mine," he said, yanking the battered door open. "Go in, stay in. I'll come for you in the morning. Door locks. I'd use it. Your cell phones'll probably work. We pirate three satellite television stations. Best one plays old movies 24/7. There's food in the cupboards. Sorry about Hannah, Amara. Sleep well."

When he was gone, Amara looked around. Man space, she decided. Single man's space, with clothes and dishes scattered, furniture duct taped and every surface dusty, except for a forty-year-old television that still had a channel dial and a chair with raven-wing arms that sat directly in front of it.

"Not bad," McVey remarked over her shoulder. "Good, actually, as it's off the beaten path."

"Way off, McVey, and a lot more beaten than any of the paths we took to get here. The word *dump* springs to mind."

He moved past her. "As long as the word *grateful* is close behind it."

"Oh, I'm grateful. Not entirely sure we'll be allowed to leave, but happy not to be spending the night with no power and the prospect of a run-in with the homicidal hit man who apparently followed us across Bellam Bridge."

"Always good to think positive, Red."

She touched a set of raven wind chimes above the TV and offered him a smile. "Also, I'm related to these people and theoretically safe from harm—on the off chance that the tales about the raven tamers turn out to be true."

McVey stowed their packs next to a lopsided sofa. "I'll have to hope my badge will be enough to get me out in one piece. And the fact that, while I did shoot Brigham, I didn't kill him."

Amara hung their rain gear on a wobbly rack, looked at the kitchen and decided she was hungry enough to check it out.

"How did Hannah die, McVey?"

"I don't think Willy Sparks had anything to do with it,

if that's what you're asking. Beyond that, her death will have to be investigated."

"Along with that second bag of coffee beans you mentioned this morning?"

"I had Jake send both bags and the brewed sample off to the county lab for analysis. Bases covered, Amara."

She opened a cupboard and, standing back, stared in astonishment. "Seriously. Brigham has soup. In cans."

"Why does that surprise you?"

"Well, duh, McVey. Look around—metaphorically speaking. Not a store in sight. I'd expect people living in such a remote area to grow herbs and vegetables, raise chickens—you know, make homemade soups, pickles and other off-the-beaten-path things."

"Maybe they're too busy teaching ravens to do tricks to worry about pickling and preserving. Anyway, I like food that comes in cans."

"That's very sad." She opened the fridge. "Okay, now, this is more what I expected. Self-bottled beer, mason jars with not-sure-what inside, and something that looks like brownies."

"Ones that'll give you a wicked case of the munchies."

Laughing, Amara closed the door and leaned back against it. "When I was a kid, Nana and my aunt—Uncle Lazarus's sister, Maureen—used to encourage me to get in touch with my Bellam side. I don't mean cast spells or brew potions…"

"Although your uncle Lazarus could present a case for the casting of spells."

"I doubt he actually thought I'd bewitched him. He just found the coincidence funny. Anyway, the point is, I got as far as being able to sense things. I'm not sure how to say this so I don't come out sounding crazy, but sometimes I could sense life, or the lack of it, in a place."

"You're talking about Bellam Manor and Hannah, aren't you?"

"There was no life inside the house, McVey. Not anywhere. Spiders don't count. Human-wise, the whole place felt—dead."

He crouched to rummage through a metal container. "You don't have to sell me on your Bellam ancestry, Red. I'm open to a fair number of beliefs. And lifestyles for that matter."

"Right. Because you weren't always a cop."

He met her questioning gaze with an unfathomable one of his own. "Were you always a doctor?"

"No, but I always wanted to be one."

"So you could make people prettier?"

"In a way." Just not the one he thought. "Talk to me about how you knew the knife guy in the days before you were a cop, McVey."

"I knew a lot of people in those days." He pulled a bottle from the container, blew off a layer of dust. "Raven's blood wine?"

"I don't see a label, so probably. How did you know him?"

He met her eyes again. "If I said the truth might shake your faith in me, would you let it go?"

A smile tugged on her lips. Circling around behind him, she set her hands on his shoulders and bent to whisper in his ear, "I'm in an RV that belongs to a raven tamer, McVey. There are stories about raven tamers that would send squeamish people like Jake's brother, Jimbo, under their beds for a week. Brigham's the only tamer I know, and I suspect he's considered affable. Hannah's dead, this storm's not moving on and we all saw someone creeping around the manor. Someone who, like us, could be stranded on this side of Bellam Bridge. There's a better than excellent chance that person is Willy Sparks. I believe you can and will deal with him, because dealing with criminals is your job. So, really, short of telling me you used to be a mass murderer, there's not a whole lot you can say about your past that'll shake my faith in you."

He turned his head just enough for her to see his expression. She couldn't read it, of course, but that was nothing new.

"I told you I was a foundling, Amara. What I didn't tell you is that the people who took me in were part of a smuggling operation."

"Part of a— Really?" She leaned farther around him. "Are you serious?"

"It was a small business, salvage items and minor artifacts from Central America. No drugs or weapons. My father had an antiques shop. My mother was his bookkeeper. I harangued them into letting me be their go-between. Everything was fine until my mother died. I was seventeen at the time. Two years later my father's heart gave out. He knew he wasn't going to make it, so he wrangled a promise from me. He wanted me to give up the life and get out before the business got out of hand. I told him I would, and I kept my word."

"You became a cop."

"Yep."

"And then?"

A smile ghosted over his mouth. "Still wearing a badge here, Red."

"Yes, but it's a Raven's Cove badge."

"What, you want me to quit and let Jake take over?"

And now they were back to evasion.

"At the risk of sounding repetitive, where does the guy with the knife enter the picture?"

He considered for a moment while lightning flickered

and fading peals of thunder echoed through the woods. "His name's Westor Hall," he said at length. "After my mother died, my father let himself be talked into expanding the business. Stakes got higher, more people got involved. Westor's sister, his father and two uncles were part of the expansion. Westor's sister died a few months ago. He thinks I turned her in. He wants to get even with me."

"So why was he holding a knife on me?"

"He saw us together. He won't hurt you, Amara. He likes to threaten, even role-play to some extent, but he's no killer. All he really wants to do is tell you about my sordid past."

"Ah. So he thinks…?" She moved a finger between them.

"It's how his mind works. You're a beautiful woman, you're with me, you must care."

A laugh tickled her throat. "What an intriguing line of reasoning." Unable to resist, she angled herself toward him. Close up, in a close space, with rain drumming on the metal roof and the windows of the RV steaming up, she suddenly found herself wanting to touch.

Somewhere inside, she knew she'd been struggling with these feelings since he'd tackled her in her grandmother's kitchen. Now here they were, all alone—well, more or less alone—in the mysterious north woods, and that struggle had become an all-out war.

She skimmed a suggestive finger over his jaw. "Tell me, McVey, just how perceptive is Westor?"

He curled the fingers of both hands lightly around her arms. "You don't want to start something with me, Amara. I can handle being a cop, but in every other way that matters, I'm a crappy risk."

The heat inside her cooled a little, but she held on to her smile. "Oh, good. So the wedding's off. Because right at the top of my to-do list was the task of seducing the new Raven's Cove police chief. Seduce, have sex, plan a relationship with, then ensnare for a lifelong commitment. After all, McVey, we've known each other a whole twenty-four hours now."

"Amara…"

"I'm not angry." But she was something, and seduction no longer played into it. She pushed at one of his hands. "I'm not upset either, or not very, which surprises me because I have a temper. Insulted, though. I'm definitely that. And I promise you, in about five seconds, if you don't let go of me, I'll work my way up to slapping your face."

"Look, you've been through a lot…"

"Yes, I have." Now she plucked his hands free one at a time. "So much so that, using typical male logic, you've decided I'm scared. Worse, you think I'm on the verge of throwing myself into your arms, and when I do, you'll feel obliged to protect me, because…well, hey, helpless female." Her eyes chilled. "I'm not Yolanda, McVey. And, yes, I know that sounds catty. It *is* catty, which must mean I'm more upset than I realized. So my mistake for starting this, and now is really not a good time to touch me."

His expression took on a suspicious edge. "Are you hysterical?"

She closed her eyes before giving in to a humorless laugh. "I'd say I have every right to be, but I'm not. I'm—" she spread her fingers "—no idea, actually. Irritated, I suppose. Frustrated."

"Mentally, emotionally or sexually?"

Her next laugh was genuine. "Okay, we are not having this conversation, right? Because, honest to God, it's way too zigzaggy for me. You say we can't start anything, yet you want to know if I'm sexually frustrated. If I say yes or even maybe—square one. So I guess no would be the appropriate— What are you doing?"

"Something I don't often do, Red." He slid the fingers of his right hand from the side around to the back of her neck. Keeping his eyes on hers, he pulled her slowly forward. "I'm changing my mind."

She refused to be tempted. Or amused. But she did meet his eyes and fist the front of his shirt. "What you said before was valid, McVey. This shouldn't happen. I have stuff, too. A past. Baggage. An ex who expected me to fall in line with his plans."

"I don't expect." As he eased in closer, anticipation pulsed through her. "All I want is for you to do the same."

"I never expect." Because his mouth was almost on hers and, hello, this was what she'd wanted all along, Amara relaxed. It was only a kiss after all.

His thumb stroked the sensitive skin below her ear. Then suddenly his hand was in her hair, his mouth was covering hers and everything inside her flipped upside down.

A single word flashed in her head. *Trouble.* It repeated, over and over again, the same word.

And it had nothing to do with Jimmy Sparks's hit man.

McVEY HADN'T MEANT to start anything, but now that he had, he couldn't stop. Couldn't think beyond the raging force of his needs.

One taste of her and he was hungry for more. Hell, he was ravenous. One touch and his brain shut down. He hadn't given up this much control since he was sixteen— more than half a lifetime ago. He'd grown jaded with time, cynical with experience—and rock hard in every possible way.

Her lips and hands yanked him right to the edge of his restraint. All he could think about was more. Of her. Of everything.

His tongue ravaged her mouth while his fingers teased the curve of her breasts.

"McVey…" She said his name as his lips slid over her jaw.

"Busy here, Red."

"I hear—music, I think."

He heard blood pounding in his head. And rain. Maybe thunder.

The pounding grew more insistent. From within it came a voice. And finally he heard the music, too.

Grasping her arms, he dragged his mouth free, swore and held them both still. "That's your phone, isn't it?"

"I can't tell. Maybe. Yes." She breathed deeply, in and out. "Yes." And turned to locate her jacket. "Someone's at the door."

He swore again, focused and heard the banging fist.

"McVey! Amara! Answer something! Phone, door, whatever!"

Amara dug out her phone and frowned. "Brigham?"

"Open the damn door!"

The latch jammed. In no mood to finesse the thing, McVey kicked the stuck metal panel until it flew outward. "What?" he demanded.

Brigham stuck a hand in, grabbed McVey's shirt and pointed with his cell. "One of the trailers fell off its blocks. The owner, Rune, went out to level it, and the whole edge of the ravine gave out. It took half the trailer down and trapped Rune underneath. I can't get to him. I'm too big and too heavy to shimmy down with a rope. But someone has to do something fast or he's a dead man."

McVey didn't think. He just took the jacket Amara shoved into his hands, said, "Show me" and went out to do his job.

THAT JOB HAD drawbacks and benefits, and McVey experienced both over the next two hours. It turned out that only Amara had been able to slide between the precariously balanced trailer and the rock wall that formed the outer edge of the ravine.

A chain of men and women had held the rope that had held him while he'd lowered her inch by inch toward the stuck man. She'd managed, after three failed attempts, to loop the end around his chest and pull it snug.

Braced just over the edge, McVey had seen her thumbs-up and pulled. Behind him, Brigham had provided a solid anchor, with everyone else holding him.

Rain had come down in sheets and caused them to slip more than once. But finally, after a grueling tug-of-war, the nightmare had ended. Several backslaps later—and after a stony once-over by a woman who looked like Mother Time—he and Amara found themselves in the well-camouflaged raven tamer barn.

Fires roared in a trio of woodstoves, tarps closed off the entire rear section and the Grateful Dead pumped from an old boom box at ear-splitting volume.

While Amara sat cross-legged on the slatted floor and put twenty stitches into the rescued man's leg, Brigham came over with two jugs of raven's blood and an assortment of mugs. He plunked his makeshift tray on a tree stump, uncorked the jugs with his teeth and poured double handed.

"Marta says you're 'common.' Means you're welcome in."

Chuckling, McVey took the mug Brigham thrust at him. "The logic being, if I'm welcome in, I'm less likely to bust anyone for whatever's behind those tarps. My guess is five or six stills and an illegal winery. Marta's a smart woman."

Brigham sampled the wine. "You don't live as long as she has by being dumb." He raised his voice, "You're common, too, Amara."

"I bet that's a first for a Bellam."

"It's a never-gonna-happen-again-Blume-blood-be-damned, so finish the patch job on Rune's leg and prepare to drink yourself stupid."

She cast an amused look in McVey's direction. "The logic being that on the off chance someone did follow us here, I'll be so ratted I won't care if my head gets blown off."

McVey sampled the bloodred wine—and found it surprisingly good. "Willy Sparks doesn't blow heads off, Amara. He'll toss you into the ravine, or try to. But he'll have to get past me and fifty raven tamers to do it." Raising his mug, and hoping like hell his system was up to the challenge, he grinned. "To being common."

THE BRIDGE WAS a nightmare. Willy made it back over, but shuddered in spasms until the lights of Raven's Hollow came into view.

The bitch was going to die in agony for this. The cop, too, for involving himself and making everything ten times harder than it should have been. Who played white knight in today's world? What kind of person put his or her own life on the line for a complete stranger? Yes, Amara was lovely, but they were talking life and death here. Cops didn't really want to die, did they?

Whether he did or not, McVey would be toast, right behind Amara Bellam. Unfortunately neither death would be taking place tonight. For the moment, they were on opposite sides of the bridge to hell.

So…what to do in Raven's Hollow that might be fun and end with a little consensual sex? When in doubt, the locals said, head to the Red Eye.

Gonna get me some tonight, Willy decided. And if the drink caused anything to slip out that shouldn't, well, more than cops and witnesses could be eliminated. What was it Uncle Jimmy liked to say? Practice made perfect.

Once again, Willy reflected, what better place to start than the Red Eye?

Chapter Eleven

"This isn't your fight, Annalee…."

The words wound through Amara's head like bright silver threads that tangled into a ball and eventually turned black. She saw a pot—a cauldron?—and smelled coffee, but no way did she plan to drink it.

The scene shifted. Where was she now?

A raven with a pink beak sat in a duct-taped chair, filing its talons.

"You're so naive, Amara," it rasped. "I told you McVey was mine. Why didn't you listen? You never listen. You're headstrong. Just like Uncle Lazarus said." One of the talons snaked out to snare her wrist. "How hard did you make him laugh…?"

Another shift, and in the swirl of thoughts flooding her mind Amara saw a woman covered in black feathers. She had Hannah's waxen features—and her lifeless green eyes. Only her mouth, thin-lipped, chalky and trembling, moved.

"Why am I in this part of the manor? Why didn't I die in my own bed?"

Like a scenery screen yanked sideways on a stage, everything changed again. The black pot that had nothing to do with Hannah popped back in. Thick red liquid bubbled up, spilled over. A woman's hand reached inside, pulled something out, held it up to look.

Amara's breath stalled. Her heart gave a single hard thump.

The hand was hers. So was the face that stared in fascination at the…whatever it was. Some kind of dripping black root.

Lips that were hers, yet not hers, moved. A voice that was definitely not hers emerged.

"Evil spirit, good spirit—no and no. Man becomes raven, yes, but the spirits that bring this transformation about are human, in action and in form. You will remember nothing of this night, Annalee…"

Amara woke with a suppressed hiss and every muscle in her body clenched like a fist. Who the hell was Annalee, and why did the name sound so familiar?

Falling back on Brigham's lumpy mattress, she regarded the dented ceiling and tried to decide if she was feeling the aftereffects of the raven's blood wine she'd consumed last night or reacting to the dream it must have spawned.

"Did you scream?"

The unexpected question had her wincing before she levered up onto her elbow.

Well, hell, her bleary mind sighed. McVey, wearing jeans and nothing else, filled the doorway of what could only be called a bedroom by virtue of the fact that there was a bed in it. One bed, four thin walls and now an über-hot cop on the threshold.

"I'm, um…"

She'd seen a half-dressed man before, right? Maybe not one who was quite so sleek and sexy, who wore his hair too long and whose sleepy eyes didn't look entirely awake, but still…

"Did you see something?" he asked. "Someone? A pink elephant?"

Amara wondered vaguely if she was wearing anything. "I think I'm good." She glanced down. Nope, not a stitch. "I had a dream. A very bizarre dream."

"Doesn't everyone who drinks devil's blood?"

"Raven's blood."

"Devil's whiskey, then."

Holding the sheet to her breasts, she regarded him with a blend of surprise and amusement. "You drank their whiskey, too—and you can walk?"

"Not especially well right now, but it'll come back to me." He'd set his hands on the door frame above his head. Whatever his condition, his dark eyes gleamed when he spied the arm banded across her chest. "This is the strangest hangover I've ever lived through, Red. I keep seeing ravens in my head. Beautiful talking ravens."

"That's because we saw talking ravens last night. Preview of coming attractions. Pretty sure they weren't real. I remember them having red eyes." She released a slow breath, rolled her head. "That wine has a wicked kick."

"You could say." McVey's pressed briefly on his eyelids. "If my brain goes south—very likely at this point—remind me when we're back on our side of the bridge to contact Lieutenant Michaels's captain as well as the county lab. If there was poison in Michaels or the coffee, I want to know about it."

"Happy thought. On a brighter note, Brigham says the raven tamers are going to do their Main Street Kickoff-to-the-Night parade on Friday."

"Yeah, I got the memo. Now that I'm 'common,' Marta informs me I'm honor bound not to notice what they'll be selling at the end-of-parade market. Or at what she's calling the preparade teaser on Thursday"

"The tamers will sell what they sell, McVey, with or without your approval. They've never had any trouble getting around Ty. And yes, I know, you're not Ty. Making you 'common' doesn't mean they'll be overt, only that they won't feel the need to post sentries. Anyway, I feel better knowing they're on our side. Now, having said that, can I please get up?"

He dropped his hands, grinned. "If you can't, I'll be more than happy to help you."

A rush of heat, Amara reflected, should not consume her because of a single suggestive remark. In fact, sex should be the furthest thing from her mind. She twirled a finger for him to turn, then stopped and nodded forward. "I believe your jeans are beeping, Chief. One, two, three, pause. One, two, three, pause…"

"You can stop the count, Red." He pulled his phone out and tapped the screen. "It's Westor."

Curious, Amara bundled the sheet around her body and scooted off the bed. "Why's he contacting you?"

"He wants to meet me tonight at the Red Eye."

"Are you sure he's not a killer?"

"He never was." McVey shrugged. "Doesn't mean he can't be bought."

She glanced through the bedroom window at the dissipating morning mist. "Why does this side of Bellam Bridge suddenly seem a lot safer to me than it did last night?"

Capturing her chin with his thumb and forefinger, McVey dropped a light kiss on her lips. "Don't get too comfortable here, Red. My observations at the manor told me that although a blow to the head was in fact responsible for Hannah Blume's death, that blow wasn't inflicted by a fall. Someone hit her."

IT GOT CRAZIER by the minute. Who would want to kill a harmless hermit of a woman?

"I'm going with a Bellam as the perp." Scowling fiercely, Jake strode back and forth at the Raven's Hollow police station. "There are loony bands of them all over the north woods. Tell me you're not thinking the same thing, McVey."

"I'm not thinking anything perp-wise. All I said was that Hannah Blume didn't fall and hit her head."

"Which you know because?" Amara asked.

He glanced up from his computer. "Any way you spin it, Red, the body position was wrong. You said yourself the blow would have killed her instantly. Means she dropped like a stone—in this case parallel to, yet away from, the corner of the counter where we found the dried blood. The facts contradict themselves."

A muscle in Jake's jaw jerked. "This bites, McVey."

Amara paced away from him. "Be glad you don't have to tell Uncle Lazarus. Be equally glad you haven't been forced to cross Bellam Bridge twice in eighteen hours. There must be another way on and off that mountain."

"Why don't you ask your new raven tamer friends?" Jake sneered. "If there's another way, they'll know about it."

She stopped pacing to frown. "Why the hostility? You're related to most of them."

"They tame ravens. That's unnatural. They brew hooch. That's illegal." He planted his hands on the desk across from McVey. "What I want to know is why we're not questioning them about Hannah's death."

"Because." McVey looked past him to Amara. "Coffee's

a negative, Red, and the forensic team on Michaels's case is still testing for toxins."

She pushed on a pressure point in her neck. "You have to figure it won't be an easy find. I need to talk to Uncle Lazarus."

"His nephew who lives with him—R.J., I think—said he was in Bangor and wouldn't be taking calls while he was gone."

"I wasn't planning to tell him about Hannah on the phone, McVey. I'll wait at his place until he gets back."

"R.J. said he might be late."

She faced him, dropped her hands. "You want me to go to the clinic, don't you?"

"It'll keep you busy."

"It'll keep me surrounded with patients."

"Patients and my deputy."

Amara told herself not to laugh at Jake's expression, which was equal parts outrage and horror.

"I've got work, McVey, over in the Cove." Jake's voice lowered. "I don't want to be around a bunch of sick people."

"You're assuming, Jake, that a bunch of sick people will magically discover there's a doctor on the premises and come flooding in."

"Word spreads fast."

"Like measles." McVey turned his attention back to Amara. "Ever since his electrical panel bit the dust six months ago, Lazarus has been living at the old Raven's Nest Motel off the even older inland highway. There's nothing else out that way."

Amara drew a mental map. "Isn't his sister's house out that way?"

"His late sister's abandoned house. The last guest at the motel signed the register back in March. He stayed for two nights and tried to skip without paying."

A nasty smile split Jake's face. "I remember that. We had us a high-speed chase that ended with him sideswiping a tree. Guy was tanked. Kept threatening to sue the tree for damages." He snickered. "As if a 1972 Pacer with bald tires and rust everywhere you looked was worth spit."

Amara rubbed her arms now. "So fond reminiscence aside, and getting back on topic, you're determined that I should hang around town for the rest of the day."

"I'm meeting the county sheriff in ninety minutes," McVey told her. "Meeting'll last at least two hours. Lazarus might or might not be home for dinner, word does spread, and as a reward for clinic duty, Jake'll be happy to hear I want him to spend the better part of his evening shift at the Red Eye."

The deputy's mouth, open to object, closed with a snap. "I guess that'll partly make up for the sickies." He stuck out a warning finger. "But I better not get measles."

Amara's eyes sparkled. "I'll give you a shot, Jake. It'll stop those measles germs in their tracks. Unless your immune system's really weak."

"Well...what if it is?"

McVey came around his desk. "Life holds few guarantees, Deputy, but here's one you can count on. Anything happens to Red between now and the next time I see her, you'll be covered in red spots. And they won't be the kind that go away."

WORD DIDN'T SO much spread as erupt. From early afternoon to early evening, Amara poked, prodded and treated more than twenty-five people, including her second cousin Two Toes Joe, who owned a dockside bar in Raven's Cove and did indeed possess only two toes on his right foot.

"Shot myself," he'd revealed, and wiggled his remaining digits. "Never point a gun at your foot if folks nearby are throwing punches. One bad bump, and *bam.*"

Having offered those words of wisdom, he'd dropped his pants and showed her his hernia.

The upside of being overrun was that time passed very quickly. Jake sulked, balked and avoided anyone who so much as coughed, but he did as ordered and stayed put in the waiting room until the last patient left.

"You tell McVey I deserve to be carried out of the Red Eye singing, Amara. Any fights break out on account of the Night or because people are as thick as twenty bricks about Hezekiah and how he came to be cursed, it's for him to handle."

"I'll pass it along."

"I don't know what all the fighting's about anyway," he grumbled. "Story's simple as Owen the Sky is Falling's brain. Nola Bellam should have stayed in the Hollow where she belonged. It wasn't Hezekiah's fault she flirted with Ezekiel and made him want her, too. And it sure as hell wasn't Hezekiah's fault he went a little crazy after Ezekiel raped her."

"So crazy that an evil spirit, who just happened to be in the vicinity, decided to help him out."

"That story's been accepted as true for a lot of years, Amara. Until some glory-seeking Bellam came along and challenged it. Put the power—good and bad—in the hands of a bunch of witches."

She smiled. "As I recall, your brother believes in that power, Jake."

"Because you scared him with your phony stories."

She packed up her instruments, said goodbye to the midwife in charge and exited the clinic ahead of him. "Guess we'll never know whether those stories were phony or the real deal, will we, seeing as Jimbo decided not to shove me off that cliff." She glanced up and around at the fog that had been rolling in for the past hour. "This stuff's getting thicker by the minute."

"It'll be pea soup before I'm done with my second glass of whiskey. Which won't be long, as the first'll be going down in a great big gulp."

"If we were talking raven tamer whiskey, you'd be the one going down, Jake—onto the floor and under the table. Do you know if McVey's back from the sheriff's office yet?"

"He's back." His expression sour, Jake walked beside her toward the noisy bar. "He said for us to meet him inside— Aw, damn, is that Lazarus going through the door?"

Amara laughed. "Oh, come on, Jake. You know Uncle Lazarus wouldn't make the same mistake…" Her denial evaporated as the fog parted to reveal Lazarus Blume's unmistakable profile. "Okay, that's me shocked."

"This night's getting crappier by the minute." Jake yanked the door open. "McVey's over talking to the bartender. I'm gonna find me a nice dark corner and crawl into it with a bottle. Let me know when the old spook of spooks leaves." With that, he vanished into the shadows.

The room was hot, crowded to the point of being barely navigable, and although Amara managed to keep McVey in sight, she lost her uncle in the first few seconds.

McVey met her halfway across the floor. "Where's Jake?" he asked above thundering Steven Earl.

"Far corner, near the washrooms." She grinned as he scouted the room. "He stuck at the clinic all afternoon, McVey, even when a seventysomething woman showed him a collection of truly hideous boils on her inner thigh."

He continued to search, but she saw his lips curve. "I'm

not looking for Jake. I'm trying to find Westor. Could be he'll go with a disguise."

"And now we add in a disguise. Does he have a favorite look?"

"He pulls off a decent old man."

"Maybe he's posing as Uncle Lazarus. Jake and I thought we saw him come in."

"He did. He's got a mad on at Yolanda. Something about cost overruns and breakage. She hightailed it. Your uncle's expression suggested her head was going to roll."

"How could you tell? His expression never changes." Not expecting an answer, Amara lifted the hair from her neck to cool it. "How did it go with the sheriff?"

"We're heading up to Bellam Manor tomorrow with full forensic and medical teams."

"Oh. That's good, I guess." Her forehead creased. "Why do I feel left out?"

"No idea. You're part of the medical team."

"I'm— What?" Mistrust swept the mild sting aside. "McVey, you know I'm not a forensic specialist. You just want me where you can see me."

"See you, feel you, touch you, Red." He draped an arm over her shoulders as the music changed from "Copperhead Road" to "Beast of Burden."

"What say we hijack a corner booth and make out until Westor shows?"

As ideas went, Amara liked it.

Or she did until glass crashed, someone screamed and the whole right side of the bar burst into flames.

WILLY HAD LEARNED from experience never to be surprised. Not by anything or anyone. But this was a shocker, and while it made no sense on the surface, logic said there had to be a reason.

Unless the person across the alley was clinically insane.

It took no more than that second of puzzled immobility for the perpetrator to turn and hesitate as Willy did. To snap an arm up as Willy did.

To shoot as Willy did....

Chapter Twelve

Fire shot from floor to ceiling. People panicked and bolted. Drinks spilled and fed the flames.

McVey knew which direction the stampede would take. He also knew the main door was already fully involved. Shouldn't be, not so rapidly, but was. Meaning this blaze had been carefully planned and executed.

He heard a bang to his right and shoved Amara down. The bartender vaulted out of harm's way as the bottled stock behind him began to crash and burn.

Amara fought the arm that restrained her. "There's an exit at the end of the corridor near the washrooms, and a delivery door in the storeroom behind the bar." She dipped down again as smoke began to blacken the air. "I think I see Uncle Lazarus. I'll get him and as many other people as possible out through the washroom corridor exit."

When a man rushing to escape knocked Lazarus Blume into a table, McVey gave up. Amara wasn't helpless, and he couldn't do it all.

"If you see Jake, tell him about the delivery door." He kissed her once, hard, then ran for the fire extinguisher on the far wall and hoped to God the cylinder was full.

AMARA KNEW SMOKE killed more effectively than fire. She used the sleeve of her jacket to cover her mouth. To reach her uncle, she had to dodge tables and chairs and at the same time try to round up as many terrified people as possible.

It didn't help that a number of them already had several drinks under their belts or that the ones who'd been playing pool were swinging their cues to clear a path through the crowd.

"Uncle Lazarus." She bent to peer at his face. "Are you hurt?"

He was doubled over a chair, gripping the back as if it were a lifeline. "Winded," he wheezed.

She wrapped an arm around his waist. "Come with me." Her voice rose. "Listen, everyone. There's a door this way. We can get out."

Slowed by her uncle's weight, she nevertheless managed to direct at least twenty people toward the little-used exit.

Her legs wanted to buckle. Lazarus Blume was not a small man, and the smoke he'd inhaled was taking its toll.

In the corridor, Yolanda burst out of the women's washroom. Half a dozen expressions raced across her face when she smelled the smoke and heard the commotion. "What's going on? What was that bang?"

"Fire in the front." Amara winced when her uncle stepped on her foot. "Help me with Uncle Lazarus."

"I can manage." Regaining his balance, he took some of his weight back.

Amara was about to release him when the people who'd rushed past them earlier backpedaled in a panic.

"Door's burning," one of the men shouted.

"We're trapped," his companion wailed.

Were they? Amara looked around her uncle at Yolanda. "Are there windows in the washrooms?"

"No—or, yes. But they're really skinny."

"We'll have to squeeze. This way," Amara said, giving

her uncle over to Benny the pharmacist. "Let the smaller people go first in case someone bigger gets stuck."

"I twisted my knee." An inebriated woman in painted-on jeans hobbled along the wall. "I can't climb."

"She goes last," Yolanda decided.

"We go last," Amara countered. "It's our uncle's bar."

"It was." Her cousin waved at the choking smoke. "Tomorrow it'll be ashes. What the hell happened? Did the gas oven blow?"

"Some kind of bomb came through the side window, I think." Amara raised her voice again. "Benny, if it's stuck, break the glass."

A few seconds later a toilet seat crashed through the window.

People climbed, crawled, wedged and wiggled through the narrow opening. When she was sure they'd reached the alley safely, Amara returned to the corridor. No way was McVey going to die because of her.

She spied Jake farther along the hall. He was hunkered down with his hand on a black pack. He surged to his feet when he spotted her—and was immediately engulfed in smoke.

Before she could take another step, Amara found herself flying—through a door and onto a tiled floor. The impact stunned her, but not as badly as the explosion in the hallway outside. The hallway she'd been standing in two seconds earlier.

McVey made sure Amara was unharmed, then, ignoring her protests, lifted her through the bathroom window. After one last foray into the inferno that was the Red Eye, he made his own escape via the smoldering delivery door.

On its own, the fog was a swirling curtain of white.

Add in plumes of black smoke and the scene around the bar went from grim to macabre.

It took several hours for volunteer firefighters to extinguish the flames.

McVey instructed the Harden twins to gather anyone in need of assistance at the clinic. Paramedics came from Bangor to help Amara treat the injured—some who'd been burned, but more, McVey suspected, who'd hurt themselves during their frantic flight.

Once the site had been taped, he posted four deputized guards and, accepting he'd done all he could, joined what Jake sarcastically referred to as "the major players" at Lazarus's Raven's Nest Motel.

They'd agreed to gather there for the simple reason that Lazarus took medication to control an erratic heartbeat and he hadn't brought it with him.

As roadside accommodations went, McVey had seen worse. On his final stakeout in New York, he'd woken up eyeball to eyeball with a rat twice the size of his fist, in a room so badly infested with cockroaches they'd crunched when he'd walked across the sagging floor.

Oh, yeah, Band-Aid-colored walls, brown carpet and a kitchenette straight out of the seventies was paradise compared to Cockroach Central.

While Louis Armstrong rasped out a tinny blues song, Lazarus sat in a straight-backed chair and listened without interruption as Amara told him about Hannah. She didn't use the word *murder,* but McVey knew they'd have to deal with that hard truth, as well. Eventually.

When she walked past him en route to her medical bag, he stopped her. "Is your uncle okay?"

"About Hannah? I can't tell. Probably not." She jabbed his stomach. "You know, you could have shouted instead of tackling me into the men's room at the Red Eye. I have excellent reflexes."

"No time." He repositioned the makeshift ice pack she'd given him when he came in—ice cubes wrapped in a towel—flexed his bruised right arm to make sure he still could and shot Jake a dark look. "I told you not to disturb any suspicious objects."

"Since when's a backpack suspicious?" Jake retorted.

"This particular pack was propped against a door with a wire running between it and the knob. In the cop world, we call that suspicious."

Lazarus batted Amara's hand away when she attempted to unbutton his jacket. "I'm not feeble, niece. I took my heart pill. It's ticking just fine." He narrowed his eyes at McVey. "Are you saying someone planted an explosive device in the rear corridor?"

"In the rear corridor, behind the bar, under one of the pool tables, above the front door. Some were on timers. Others were rigged to blow if moved."

"In other words," Lazarus said, "we're dealing with a mass murderer."

Amara plucked a piece of glass from his collar. "That murderer has a name, Uncle. It's Willy Sparks."

Seated on the floor, knees pulled up, arms tightly folded around them, Yolanda speared Amara with a vicious look. "This is your fault. You brought it here. Danger. Death. Bombs. And now, because we were all shaken and stupid and wanted to get out of town in case the whole main street blew up, we rushed to the back of beyond— no offense, Uncle Lazarus—to try to sort out what most of us already knew but were too rattled to realize until we got here."

"She means we're sitting ducks." Jake flung an angry arm. "And damn it, she's right. Who says this Willy Sparks person you told us about won't decide to come barreling through the front window in a truck loaded with explosives?"

"He does that, he'll be dead right along with us." Lazarus searched his pockets. "I need a pink pill. R.J. knows where all my medications are. Where is he?"

"I sent him up to the roof." McVey watched the fog. "He won't see anything coming, but he might hear it."

"He's a good man." Lazarus patted his inside pockets. "Ex-army. I was sure I brought them with me."

"You take two kinds of heart medication?" Amara asked.

"I take antacid, the pink kind, when I eat shellfish for dinner." His shoulders slumped. "I was fond of Hannah in my way. She amused me with tales about Hezekiah and his transformation when I was young. When I got a little older, she taught me to play chess on the raven board her grandfather carved by hand and passed down to her."

Amara rubbed his arm. "I'll check the medicine cabinet for that antacid."

Unable to see through the fog, McVey followed her to the bathroom.

"Who lives in a motel?" She yanked the mirrored cabinet door over the sink open and almost off its hinges. "Before you answer, McVey, I know his home electrical panel shorted out."

He rested a shoulder on the door frame. "Good electricians are hard to find, Red."

The quick play of emotions on her face fascinated him. It also made him hungry for another taste of her. He bridged the gap between them in half a stride, cupped the back of her head and brought her gaze up to his. "This isn't your fault, Amara."

A hollow smile grazed her lips. "Of course it is. I ran

and hid, or tried to, in a place where people I love live. It wouldn't have been much of a brain strain for Jimmy Sparks to have considered the possibly and send his—whatever Willy is—to Maine to check it out. And wonder of wonders, here I am."

"That's Yolanda talking. And Jake. Yes, word does spread quickly in small towns, but from what I've heard about your day, no one who came to the clinic was worried that he or she would be taking a bullet on your behalf. Story I got was that you were swamped."

"That's just people in need weighing risk against discomfort and deciding that a few minutes of the first are worth a lessening of the second." She wrapped her fingers around his wrist. "Are you sure nobody was killed tonight?"

"Firefighters went through the wreckage, Amara. There were no bodies. You and the paramedics patched up eleven people who were cut by flying glass and three who suffered minor burns. No one showed any serious signs of smoke inhalation, and I've seen more scrapes and bruises after a weekend bar brawl than I did tonight."

"Hmm." Taking his hand from her face, she hunted through the medicine cabinet for antacid tablets. She found them behind two large vials and an old-fashioned shaving brush. Staring at the bristles, she said, "Why would Willy blow up an entire bar, McVey? It's out of character—if he has a character." A breath shuddered out. "I want him to stop."

"I know."

"Do you think that's the point? He's pissed off because he wants the job done and it's not getting done?"

"Maybe." McVey prevented her from leaving by trapping her arms as she tried to pass him. "You're forgetting something, Amara."

"Pretty sure I'm not."

"Hannah." He said it simply and had the satisfaction of seeing her eyes snap to his. "Willy Sparks didn't kill her. The time frame's off and, like the bar fire tonight, so's the M.O."

She let her forehead fall against his shoulder. He thought she probably wanted to bang it there. "I'm so confused. It's as if there's this huge disco ball in my brain where thoughts, ideas, facts, you name it, bounce off the mirrored pieces into the dark. How am I supposed to collect and process all of them?"

He kissed her hair. "Collecting and processing is my job, Red. You treat cuts and burns and make the world a prettier place."

"Is that a crack about the surgeries I perform?"

"Nope, it's an observation." He tipped her head up and kissed her just long enough to make himself hard. Not the brightest thing he could have done. Stepping back, he kissed her one more time and said, "It's way past late. I have a lot of rubble to dig through in the morning and a mountain to scale in the afternoon."

She regarded him through her lashes. "What aren't you telling me, McVey?"

"I can't answer that until I find out what Westor didn't tell me. I'm not holding my breath it'll be worth anything, but you never know. In the meantime, you know the drill."

A reluctant smile appeared. "Bet you wish you'd stayed in New York."

"Trust me, Amara. An unarmed midnight stroll through Central Park would be a piece of cake compared to this mess." He nodded at the bottle in her hand. "Take those to your uncle. It's time we headed back to your grandmother's place. Instincts I've learned to trust, but don't necessarily like, are telling me tomorrow could be a day worse than anything either of your ancestral families ever faced."

IF HIS INSTINCTS were even half-correct, Amara wanted no part of the coming day. Not the postdawn tromp around the blackened shell of her uncle's bar, and definitely not the trip up Bellam Mountain to fetch Hannah Blume's body down to Raven's Cove.

It relieved her that the morning promised good weather. Somewhere between the time they'd left the motel and that lovely moment when she'd toppled facedown onto her bed, the fog had rolled out to sea. It said a great deal about her state of exhaustion, Amara reflected, that she hadn't performed her habitual when-in-Grandma's-house spider check before she fell.

Not trusting the sunny weather to hold, she dressed in snug jeans, comfortable hiking boots, a white tank and a scarlet jacket. Birds and deer got shot in the woods. She didn't intend to.

McVey wisely suggested they buy their morning coffee at a nearby filling station en route to the Hollow. Until they'd taken their first sips, neither of them spoke beyond a grunt. Then reality slithered in.

Pulling herself onto the running board, Amara regarded McVey over the top of his truck. "Am I right in thinking that you're thinking the same person who killed Hannah might have planted those explosives at the Red Eye?"

McVey set his coffee cup on the roof to shrug out of his jacket. "I'm thinking lots of things, Red. That's one of them."

"Score one for the noncop." She waited a beat before asking, "Why?"

"Because, as you said last night, murdering a room

full of innocent people isn't Jimmy Sparks's M.O. He's all about family. His own first and foremost, but word has it, he's very discriminating when it comes to murder. Choose a target, hit a target. Deviate when necessary, but order Willy to blow up a bar filled with people who might or might not be related to you? Not his style."

"Plus, Willy couldn't have been sure I'd be there, and several of those devices must have been planted either before or shortly after the Red Eye opened. Bringing me full circle to totally confused."

"You're not alone." He flipped his sunglasses down, climbed in. "Let's go find some answers."

Amara was fastening her seat belt when she heard the distant report of a rifle.

Hunters was her first thought. But two more blasts followed by a pause, followed by three more blasts and another pause had prickly knots forming in her stomach.

Before the final three shots sounded, McVey had the truck started and the front end pointed back toward her grandmother's house.

When he braked at the edge of the woods, Amara turned to face him. "Don't even think about telling me to stay here."

"Not planning to. I'm guessing those shots came from the tortured oaks. Gun." He pointed to the glove box, then climbed out and, with his Glock shoved in his waistband, removed an AK-47 rifle from the locked box in the back.

Fear skated along Amara's spine. "Okay, so…not taking any chances."

"Not anymore. Stay right on my heels, Amara. Anyone comes up behind you, spin and shoot. Can you do that?"

"It goes against the Hippocratic oath, but yes, I can."

"You've got balls, Red." He used the rifle to gesture. "This way."

They left the main trail almost immediately and forged their own faster path through the trees. At one point, Amara found herself knee-deep in brush on terrain only a goat would deem traversable.

The shots were much closer when they repeated—less than fifty yards to her left.

The tortured oaks, the personification of agonized death, came into sight behind a clump of pines. Nothing and no one stirred in the small clearing. Stray beams of sunlight sliced through the pointed rocks like crossed swords.

McVey went down on one knee. Amara knelt beside him and strained to hear what she couldn't see.

"There's a lot of birdsong," she noted. "Animals scrabbling. Insects chirping." Closing her eyes, she took a deep breath and held it.

She caught a rustle and under it, a barely audible moan. "There." Opening her eyes, she touched McVey's arm. "In the scrub behind the second oak."

He didn't question, merely reached for his Glock and used it to draw an invisible arc from their current position to the tree.

Birds tweeting for mates masked their footsteps. Amara willed her heart to stop its frantic thudding. Hyperventilating wouldn't help the situation.

The scrub shifted. She heard a cough. Gurgly, she thought, and kept her gun angled skyward.

"I don't think he's baiting us," she whispered. "He has fluid in his lungs."

With the tip of his rifle, McVey parted the bushes. She spied a gleam of metal before he blocked her from sight with his body.

"Drop it, Westor," he warned, "or you're a dead man."

Propped against the base of a chestnut tree, Westor let out a wet laugh and lowered his arms.

"Not a problem, old friend." Blood glistened on his teeth when he smiled. "I'm a dead man already."

Chapter Thirteen

"I need my medical bag."

But even as Amara started to stand, McVey slung the rifle over his shoulder and prevented her from leaving. "It's too late."

Helplessness clawed at her. "There must be something we can do." She tore at the bloody front of Westor's shirt—and knew the moment she saw the wound that McVey was right. The hole, less than an inch below the man's heart, oozed blood every time he coughed.

McVey stopped his head from lolling. "Talk to me, Westor." A firm shake kept him from slipping under. "Come on, old friend, don't let whoever did this to you get away with it."

Westor's eyes rolled. "The alley…it was… Oh, man. Hurts like a bitch. Hot knives, you know?" He clutched McVey's arm. "Bury me with mine," he said clearly.

"Try not to move," Amara told him gently. He slumped back, smiled again and set his half-open eyes on her face. "Never be a witness…" The words slurred and overlapped. He trailed off, still smiling.

"He's dead." Amara double-checked the pulse in his neck. "I'm sorry, McVey."

"I imagine he is, too."

"He mentioned an alley. If he meant the alley behind

or beside the Red Eye, it would have taken him hours to get here from there. I mean, he obviously did it, but…"

"Yeah. But." McVey closed Westor's eyes. "Do you have a signal on your cell?"

She checked. "No."

"We'll have to leave him. I'll contact the sheriff from my truck, tell him to bring extra men. The Hardens are on duty in the Hollow today. Dean, my junior deputy, can handle the Cove."

Amara stood. "Do you think this is Willy Sparks's or our mysterious other killer's doing?"

"I'm leaning toward the mysterious other myself."

"He's starting to terrify me more than Willy." She stared down at Westor. "How is that possible?"

McVey set a hand on the back of her neck and gave her a reassuring squeeze. "There's a reason for everything that's happening, Amara. It's a matter of connecting one dot to the next and seeing if we're looking at a single large picture or two smaller ones."

Amara said nothing, just watched in thoughtful silence as a raven swooped down to perch on a broken branch.

In Raven's Cove, three raven's feathers placed on a door meant the person to whom the door belonged was destined to die. She didn't know what a staring raven might mean. She only knew this was the second time she'd noticed one watching her.

And her Blume blood recognized the potential significance of this one doing so from a point directly above a dead man's head.

LESS THAN AN hour later McVey was wading through the scorched debris that had once been the Red Eye. Little remained of the bar except the walls, and the chief inspector had declared them to be highly unstable. No one would be allowed near the burn area.

Businesses on both sides had suffered major smoke and water damage. That meant there'd be no barber service or Chinese takeout in the foreseeable future.

After a long chat with the inspector, McVey posted guards in shifts and went in search of Amara at the clinic. She'd gone there when seven-months-pregnant Megan Bellam—undoubtedly a cousin—had asked her for more detailed medical advice than the midwife could supply.

Amara was drying her hands on a towel as he came in. "If you've got a crappy mood going, McVey, listen to a baby's heartbeat and all's well with the world. Megan's having a girl."

"Nola's line or Sarah's?"

"Nola's. In an ode to Edgar Allan, plus the fact that her daddy's got Blume blood, they're going to call her Lenore."

"Excellent news on all fronts. Now, at the risk of bursting your baby-heartbeat bubble, it's time for us to gear up and head out."

"From death to life to death." She hoisted her medical bag onto her shoulder. "Will we be spending the night on Bellam Mountain?"

He let her precede him through the clinic door and into the brilliant May sunshine. "Depends how the investigation unfolds. If it's down to you and me, we can stay at Hannah's. There are some fairly cool rooms in her wing."

"I'm told she was a fairly cool woman. Sort of Katherine Hepburn-esque in her prime."

"More Mother Goose-ish in her later years."

"I think the Mother Goose comparison came from the fact that she made up kiddie rhymes about the local legends. I only remember one—

'Red eyes, black feathers. Once a man,

But now a raven. Evil can
No longer feed on wretched soul,
And yet shall ever take its toll
On Hezekiah Blume. And all
Who share his blood, will share his fall...."'

"I wouldn't call that especially kiddie-like."

"It is if you live in the Cove or the Hollow. Did you talk to the sheriff about Westor?"

McVey nodded. "He's sending some people to retrieve the body. We didn't kill him, Amara. Remember that. And whoever did will pay." When his phone beeped, he reached into his jeans, pulled it out and hit Speaker. "What is it, Jake?"

"It's a pair of frigging feet's what it is. I was moving a nosy Parker along and he tripped. Fell on some trash bags. He started flailing because they smelled bad. When he got clear's when I saw the feet." Jake's voice tightened. "They ain't moving, McVey, and they ain't the right color, either. I'm thinking we got us a corpse."

SHE'D BEEN UP since 6:00 a.m., Amara reflected. Barely four hours. And already two people were dead.

She spotted Jake squatting in a sea of green trash bags and carefully made her way with McVey into the side alley.

"Report, Deputy," McVey said as they got closer.

Her cousin looked up. "She's dead."

Amara skirted him, hoping for a clearer view.

"Her face is familiar." Jake screwed his own up. "I just can't place it."

"Mina." Amara knelt beside the body. "That's her name. Mina Shell. She was in the pharmacy the day Westor grabbed me. He grabbed her, too...." She bent closer. "What's that in her hand?"

McVey shifted the green bag that partially covered the

woman's right arm. "A rag stuffed in a bottle. It's a Molotov cocktail. The one that started the fire was tossed through the window at the street end of the alley."

Puffing hard, the sheriff, a short, potbellied man, joined them. "Is this the firebomber, then?"

Because she was closest, Amara sniffed the rag. Over the odor of rotting trash, she caught the distinct smell of gasoline. "I am so lost." She sighed. "Mina said she came here for the Night of the Raven, but what she really intended to do was blow up the Red Eye? Why?"

"Gonna have to leave that one for now, Red." McVey moved more of the bags. "She's wearing a watch on her right wrist. And her left thumbnail's shorter than the right, possibly for texting purposes. She could be left-handed."

"What difference does that make?" Jake frowned when McVey didn't answer. "Does it make a difference?"

Amara sat back. "She's holding the bottle in her right hand, Jake. If she planned to throw it, shouldn't it be in her left?"

"You saying it was put there after she was dead?" Jake's frown deepened. "By who?"

"Whoever firebombed the Red Eye." McVey shrugged. "Theoretically."

Amara thought back to the pharmacy. "I think—I'm not sure, but I think—Mina reached for the lipstick with her left hand. Having said that, of course, she might have been holding the bomb in one hand with the intention of switching it to and throwing it with the other."

McVey ran his gaze over the body. "I only see one entry wound. One shot, middle of her throat. Someone knows how to kill quickly and efficiently."

"Someone like Willy Sparks." Amara assumed. She rubbed a sudden chill from her arms. "Westor said, 'Never be a witness.' He must have seen this happen, or certainly something that happened here last night."

Jake slashed a hand in front of him. "Wait a minute. Are we saying this woman did or didn't throw the first Molotov cocktail through the window?"

"We're saying we don't know who did what to whom, when or in what order. Yet." McVey regarded the portly sheriff. "It's your call, Walt. Do you want to stay here with this or make the trip up to Bellam Manor?"

"Best if I stay and you take the teams up. I'm a damn sight better at solving murders than I am at navigating shaky bridges."

While they talked, Amara regarded Mina's lifeless body. Three people were dead, and only one of those deaths made any kind of sense to her.

Like Hannah's, Mina's glassy eyes looked up at nothing. Her mouth hung open and there was a smear of pink lipstick on her upper teeth.

Had she and Westor simply been in the wrong place at the wrong time? Had they been in that place separately or together? Stranger things had happened, and for all his leers and lewd remarks, Westor had been a hot-looking man. Maybe Mina had slept with him— And where the hell, Amara wondered, was she going with that idea?

Not a cop, she reminded herself.

She tuned back in when McVey came up behind her.

"Time to roll, Red. The sheriff's got this one. We're down a few people on each team, but we'll manage. Hannah's death needs investigating as much as Mina's."

"And Westor's."

"His, too." McVey held her gaze. "I don't want anyone else winding up in the morgue."

Amara nodded. She needed quite badly to believe that no one else would die. But in her mind, she saw the raven watching her from a branch above Westor's body while a dead man's last words echoed eerily in her head.

Never be a witness....

THE DRIVE UP Bellam Mountain was nothing next to the step-and-cling crossing of Bellam Bridge. McVey took the less-encumbered team members up the steep stone path. Amara and the others made the longer trek to the manor via the twisty access road.

The unseasonably hot day had turned out muggier than expected. McVey hadn't moved Hannah's body, and the central kitchen's windows faced north. It would have received a strong dose of morning sun.

A note from Brigham on the door told him the big raven tamer had been watching the manor. No one had come near the place or attempted to disturb the body, making it unlikely in McVey's opinion that they'd find a murder weapon. Still, procedure dictated that a full-scale search be undertaken.

Amara arrived twenty minutes later. She wore his Dodgers baseball cap, oversize sunglasses and had her jacket tied around her waist. His blood did a lot more than stir when she herded her group into the manor and he caught the subtle scent of her perfume.

This was death and a decomposing body. He had no business thinking about Amara's soft skin, her silky hair or how her mouth would taste. And it seemed just plain weird to wonder what it would feel like to make love to her in the grass next to the pond they'd passed the other night on the way to the raven tamers' camp.

Thankfully, his iPhone beeped as the last few team members passed between them. He kept his eyes on Amara's face when he answered on speaker. "More problems, Jake?"

"We can't find her purse."

McVey had to kick-start his brain. *Her* could only be Mina Shell. "How large an area have you searched?"

"Most of the alley. Sheriff made me call up to Blume House. She's not registered there."

"She could have been camping."

"Maybe, but not at the Ravenspell campsite."

"Run her name through the DMV, see what comes up. Has Westor's body been recovered yet?"

"Just." The deputy grunted. "Think I might know where he was flopping. There's an empty apartment in Yolanda's building. Turns out maybe she wasn't harboring a fugitive after all. The lock on the empty place was jimmied, and the Hardens found stuff on the floor. Food wrappers, wine bottles, sleeping bags, a .30-30 rifle, a couple boxes of bullets."

"Dust for prints and keep me informed about the woman." McVey signed off. "What?" he asked when he saw Amara drawing an air picture.

"I'm thinking back." Her brows came together. "She didn't have paper or a pen. I tore off a sheet of paper and gave it to her. That's when Westor grabbed me—us."

"And translated that means?"

"I told you earlier, Mina found the lipstick she wanted behind the cosmetics counter in the pharmacy. She picked it up with her left hand, but even more significant, she took the pen I gave her with the same hand. That still doesn't prove she wasn't simply holding the bomb bottle in her right hand, though, does it? Ah, except..." She swung around. "That's not the point. The point is, why would Mina want to set fire to the Red Eye in the first place? We're saying the bottle might have been planted on her to deflect suspicion from the real firebomber."

"Head of the class, Red."

"With a detour you apparently didn't take." Smiling, she strolled up to him and tapped a finger to his chest. "Guess that's why you wear the badge."

"Lucky me."

"The day's young. We'll see." She kissed him so thoroughly that bullets of lust shot off in multiple directions. He started thinking perfume, skin, sex and, oh, yeah, pond all over again.

Unfortunately she stepped away before he could pursue any of those thoughts. "Back in the real world, what's happening with Hannah?"

A picture of the older woman's body flashed in McVey's head. No question, there were times when a grisly visual was far more effective than a cold shower. "Let's say she's looking a little less healthy than the last time you saw her."

"He means she's gone gray and putrid."

Brigham approached from the side. His arrival wouldn't have surprised him, McVey reflected, if he hadn't let the idea of sex with Amara tie his senses in knots.

"We're heading down to the Hollow." The big man jerked a thumb. "Taking our ravens and our bits and pieces for the street show/parade with us. You figure on spending the night up here?"

McVey glanced at his phone. "It's almost two o'clock. I'd say there's a fair chance."

"Everyone or just you and Amara?"

"Just us. The teams know the way back."

"Uncle Lazarus asked me to pick up a number of Hannah's personal effects and bring them down," Amara said. "Mostly small items. Some of them might be tricky to find."

"Yeah, well, just so you know, the rain's coming back."

She held her smile at Brigham's dire prediction. "Of course it is. Because legends rule here, and according to one of them, it always rains at night up on Bellam Mountain. Has to be Sarah's doing. What else would a mad witch jailed in an attic room do but put nasty spells on everything she could think of?"

Brigham gave her a deliberate once-over. "You being her offspring, so to speak, and common to us tamers now, maybe you could spend a few minutes working out how to stop the wet. One more mudslide and we'll have to move our camp."

Which they probably did every few years in any case. But right then McVey had weightier problems to handle in the form of three murders, no solid leads and still way too much sex on the brain.

He used the familiar routine of police work to combat the latter. But four frustrating hours into it, they still hadn't turned up a single piece of evidence in or around the murder scene.

"She died where she fell." The head of the forensic team wiped a grimy arm across his face. "Blood loss tells us that much even without a weapon. Seeing that leg of hers, though, I can't imagine why she came to this derelict part of the manor. It's a head-scratcher, McVey, and that's a fact."

Another fact, McVey noticed when he took a moment to look outside, was that Brigham's forecast had been dead-on. Black clouds were massing over the water, and they appeared to be creeping inland.

It took the better part of another hour to stretcher and bind Hannah's body, then pack the equipment for the return trip. Once the teams were ready, McVey secured the central core, separated Amara from her new physician friends and pulled her toward the more livable west wing.

Digging in, she glanced behind them. "There must be more we can do here, McVey."

He kept a firm hold on her hand and a close eye on the clouds. "There's more, Amara. It just can't be done in the dark or by us alone. Brigham left some wine, you want to go through Hannah's things, and I want a shower before whatever's blowing in with those clouds knocks the power out for the better part of the night...." Mild impatience brought his brows together. "Why are you dragging your feet?"

"Because I'm superstitious enough not to like what's sitting on the lamppost outside Hannah's door."

"You're half Blume and you don't like ravens?"

"One raven's not a problem. Two, I can deal. Three starts to freak me out." She continued to resist his pull. "Is it staring at me?"

"If it is, and it's a boy bird, it has excellent taste. If what you really want is for me to shoot it, tell me so we can get inside the damn house."

She twisted her hand free. "You don't shoot a raven, McVey, or anything, for staring." Her declaration ended on a shiver. "I knew this would happen. I'm letting the legends get to me. It's the curse of being a Bellam-Blume. You get swept up."

"There's a thought," he said, and, sweeping her into his arms, carried her past the watchful bird. "What do you know?" He deposited her on the porch. "You're still alive."

"And kicking," she said, but left it at a cool verbal threat rather than a physical demonstration. "First shower's mine. You'll want to batten down the hatches. And the shutters." When he narrowed his gaze, a smile blossomed. "Add my warning to Brigham's and heed it. With the thunder will come strong winds." Stepping closer, she stroked a deliberate finger from his cheekbone to the corner of his mouth. "Trust me, McVey, however many storms you've experienced since you arrived in the Cove, this one will top them all."

His eyes glinted in the shadowy half light. "Are you trying to convince me that you're a witch or frighten me with your ominous prediction?"

Letting her hand fall, she hooked his waistband and tugged him forward. "I'm not a witch, McVey, I'm a woman." She turned her face up to his. "And right now I want."

He thought he detected a rumble of thunder and maybe a warning burst of wind. But all he really heard was the rush of blood in his head and the roar of it in his ears. He felt it pulsing in his groin as her mouth fused itself to his and hurled him—hurled them—into a far more frightening fire than the one they'd taken on last night.

Chapter Fourteen

Amara intended to get what she wanted—hot, steamy sex, with a hot, sexy cop. She didn't care where it took place. Outside, inside, on the floor, on a bed, on the table. She wanted McVey's mouth on her mouth, his body pressed against hers and his hands anywhere at all.

Desire curled inside as he took her by the hips and brought her up to him. More than heat pumped from his body. She felt need as well, raw and unbridled, with an edge as keen and urgent as her own.

Her back bumped the door. Then that door was gone and a cloud of warmth engulfed her. But the real burn was in her belly, in her blood, in the hands that glided with abandon down his chest to the front of his jeans.

"This isn't how I thought it would be." Her breath unsteady, she obliged him by letting her head fall back and exposing her throat to his lips.

"If slow was the goal, Red, we started off all wrong." He eased away just far enough to fix his dark eyes on hers. "Jumping you that first night planted a seed inside me I haven't been able to exorcise."

She teased him with a smile. Her hand slid to his lower belly. "I'm sure you can imagine. I'm all about exorcism. Or possession, depending on how you look at it."

"Right now I'm looking at you."

Her hand tightened on the front of his jeans. "Excellent response, McVey."

The shifting shadows played across his features. His eyes grew darker in the changeable light. He ran his hands under her tank top, brushed callused palms over her bare skin. When his thumbs grazed her lace-covered nipples, Amara hissed in a breath of pure pleasure. And laughed it out when he took hold of her hips and this time lifted her right off her feet.

She wrapped her legs around him in a move that was as much reflex as desire.

Excitement leaped inside her. The pulse at the base of her throat throbbed. He pressed his lips to the delicate hollow and she bowed her body toward him, determined to absorb as many sensations as possible.

"Are we moving, or have my head and body separated?" With her eyes firmly shut, she summoned a feline smile. "More to the point, am I talking or dreaming?"

"Talking." McVey explored every part of her mouth. "I like it. I like your voice. It haunts me. I hear it in my sleep."

"You hear…" Her lashes flew up. Her heart continued to pound and her breathing was far from steady, but she couldn't let that pass. "I'm not her, McVey. Not the woman from your dream."

"Nightmare." He corrected and then kissed her so thoroughly she almost lost the thread of her objection. Did lose it for a blissful moment. "It's your voice I hear, Amara. I never wanted her."

Need gathered in a fiery ball in her belly. When he brought her up higher, it speared outward to her limbs and took most of the air in her lungs with it.

Darkness and light collided. Wind whipped the turbulent clouds into a frenzy. Stairs groaned; the floor creaked. Amara kept McVey's mouth busy and at the same time used her hands to touch and savor and hold. To push him to the limit and that one step beyond.

He laid her on something soft—a mattress?—and, freeing his mouth, stared down at her.

"Gotta get you naked, Red, while I can still form a thought."

If he could form thoughts, he was far ahead of her.

Her lips curved and she willed her hazy eyes to focus. Bed, walls, window, storm. McVey undressing her while her own fingers worked feverishly on the fly of his jeans. She tugged and dragged and tossed. She felt air; the hot, muggy weight of it on her skin as he pulled the white tank top over her head and cupped her breasts.

"Beautiful," he murmured.

Leaving her lace bra in place, he lowered his mouth to her nipple. She arched her back in reaction, heard the purr of approval that came from deep in her own throat.

Her fingernails bit into his shoulders, raked along his upper arms. She was lost and not looking to find herself any time soon. The torture of foreplay was too delicious to rush, the need for more exquisitely painful.

Heat and hunger throbbed in her veins. The combination threatened to consume her. The fire at the Red Eye had nothing on what burned inside her right now.

She fed on McVey's mouth as he slid his hand lower over her belly. He swallowed the gasp she couldn't contain when he slipped that hand between her legs and began to stroke her.

In a move as swift as the first streak of lightning, Amara took the full, hard length of him in her fingers and brought him with her to the slippery rim.

She felt his jerk of reaction. "You don't play fair, do you, Red?"

Her entire system jittered. "Fair's not in my genes." To

prove it, she gripped him tighter. And through her lashes had the satisfaction of seeing his eyes darken to near black.

The image lingered long after her vision wavered, until all that remained was a wash of color as she streaked toward that lovely peak.

When she brought him inside her, when he filled her, she clenched around him and held fast.

"Now, McVey. Right now!" She gasped the words, might have shouted them, because, for a moment, every part of her seemed to fly, to race through the night like the approaching thunderbolts.

In her mind she found the source of the lightning and grabbed it. Rode on its wild, electric back through the sky. Then it vanished. Her muscles went limp, her arms fell away and she tumbled slowly back into herself.

Now, that, her dazed and bleary mind managed to reflect, was what she called a wicked light show. And now she drifted on a sea of black raven's feathers.

She had the ancestry for it. Ravens didn't necessarily foreshadow death in the Bellam world. On that side of her family tree, the birds were often harbingers of hope. And to some degree, she supposed, love.

"Did you say something?"

McVey sounded the way Amara felt—spent, dazed and thoroughly sated. He lay facedown on the bed with his face buried in the pillow and her hair. The arm he'd slung over her held her firmly in place, or would have if she'd had the energy to move even one muscle.

"Not sure I'm up to talking yet." The illusion of drifting resumed when she closed her eyes. "Is my body vibrating or is the house shaking?"

He raised his head to glance at the window before propping up on his elbows. "Likely some of both. The sky's a light show."

"So's my mind. That was—amazing. I swear I saw stars."

"I think I blacked out."

She laughed. "Before, during or after?"

"Take your pick." A smile tugged on his mouth and, lowering his head, he took hers again.

Her heart, not yet back to its normal rhythm, threatened to hammer out of her chest. She hooked a leg over his hips and moved against him in sly, suggestive circles.

Sliding his lips over her cheek, he chuckled. "Need a minute here, Red. I'm still working my way down."

"I know it." This time she ravaged his mouth. When she was done, her eyes glittered. "What do you say to a change of pace? Not that I don't love fast and furious, but building from slow and easy might be nice."

"Might be," he agreed. "But I think…" Catching her waist, he rolled her on top of him so her legs straddled his lower belly. "I want to see you with lightning flashing around your head, then streaming down over your body."

The slyness spread to Amara's eyes. Leaning closer, she whispered a teasing, "In that case, McVey, I hope you're well-grounded. Because the storm out there is a spring shower compared to what's in store for you in here."

THE WORLD AS McVey knew it gave a mighty quake. His eyes snapped open to shadows. The floor beneath him threatened to buckle and the air was rich with the mingled smells of smoke and storm.

A fire, tinged with green, flamed high in an impossibly tiny hearth. A small black pot hung over the flames. Three others stood smoking on a heavy table.

A woman in a cloak moved from pot to pot. She mumbled and chanted and sprinkled powders that made the contents boil over the sides. "Betray me and suffer the consequences," she vowed. "What was love has transformed into hate. I pit brother against brother and seek destruction for both. At night's end, all that the first one possesses shall pass to me and mine."

"Go!" Whirling, she held her hands out, palms up. As they rose, so did the flames in the hearth. Her voice dropped to a malevolent whisper. "Never forget, Hezekiah. It was your own brother who killed your wife—your wife, who was my sister. He raped her and then he killed her. He betrayed us both, for I loved him, and I foolishly believed he loved me."

Fury smoldered in the air. Vicious streaks of lightning revealed more than a desire for revenge in her eyes. From the floor where he lay, unmoving and with his own eyelids barely cracked, McVey saw the madness that simmered inside her.

"All will be mine," the woman promised again. "Before this night is done, there will be death many times over, and the perpetrator shall be deemed to be evil…."

Her words echoed in McVey's head. Echoed and expanded. In his mind he saw a man. There was blood, and suddenly the man was alone with bodies scattered across the forest floor. His brother lay dead at his feet. His breath heaved in and out, and tears ran down his cheeks as he cried a woman's name.

"Nola…!"

The smoke in the attic thickened. The storm beyond it grew wilder still. But in the forest of his mind, McVey glimpsed a raven. It swooped down and landed in front of the sobbing man. It spread its silky black wings and grew to full human size.

When it spoke to him, it did so in a woman's soft voice. "I can do but a small spell, my love, yet I shall do all that is possible to save what remains of your soul. You must embrace the raven, Hezekiah. You must embrace and become the raven....

The image in McVey's head fractured. He saw fire and blood and the dripping black mass that the cloaked woman had given to the damned man.

But it was fragments now; frozen images caught in time-lapse photography.

He had to get out, McVey thought. He had to do something. Find someone. No, protect someone. Protect Amara from the person who wanted her dead.

Without warning, the woman's strong fingers gripped his wrists and hauled him to his feet. "I knew you were awake, Annalee. I know what you have seen and heard. I know what you think."

McVey seriously doubted that. How could a mad witch know the thoughts of a man who was, however briefly and for whatever reason, trapped inside the body of her sister Nola's daughter?

"MCVEY, WAKE UP!" He felt himself being shaken—not by the wrists, but by the shoulders. "McVey!"

The female voice, muted at first, came clearer. She shook him again, then committed the cardinal sin of wrapping her fingers around his wrist.

"McVey!"

Hell with that, he thought and, yanking free, took a hard swing.

"Not tonight, slugger."

His fist punched air. The momentum of it landed him facedown on a dusty floor.

Weight descended on the small of his back. Firm bands cinched his ribs on either side. A hand grabbed his hair and pulled.

"Wake up!" a familiar voice said in his ear.

Reality trickled in, slowly at first, then like a bucket of ice water dumped over his head.

He came back swearing and reaching for his gun. When he surged up, the weight vanished. He made it to his hands and knees, looked around—and saw Amara sprawled on the floor.

Concern struck first, a brutal kick to the gut. "Are you hurt? What are you doing?" He shoved himself upright, swayed. "What am I doing?" His mind began to clear and he frowned. "Where the hell are we?"

"All good questions." She pushed to a crouch to study his face in the shadowy light. "Are you *you*?"

The dream—hell, nightmare—slithered back in. So did a truckload of confusion. "I don't know who I am, or was. Is this an attic?"

She continued to inspect his face. "Yes. We're in the central part of the manor. I woke up when you got out of bed and pulled on your jeans. No big deal, I thought. Until the lightning flickered and I saw your eyes. They looked wrong. Trancelike. I called your name, but you didn't answer. When I touched you, you shoved me onto the bed."

"I shoved…?" Revulsion swept through him. "Jesus, Amara, did I hurt you?"

"Onto the bed, McVey. No. I tried to follow you, but you're very fast, and when I realized you were heading outside, I had to run back for my boots."

And his T-shirt, he noted. "Your hair's wet."

"It's raining. And blowing. Hard. I don't know how I knew you'd gone to the main part of the house. Maybe I sensed you. Or maybe it just made some kind of weird sense to me that you'd come here, but I ran upstairs when I heard the attic door slam."

"I hope it was me who made that happen and not the house."

She smiled. In relief, he imagined.

"I don't think the manor's possessed, McVey, but the central attic is believed to be where Sarah Bellam was confined after she was pronounced insane."

"Insane and pregnant."

The smile spread to Amara's eyes. She held her hands out to her sides. "Tah-dah."

"With Ezekiel Blume's child."

"Thus the sparsely populated branch that binds our family trees."

McVey lowered his gaze to his forearms. "She grabbed me, dragged me to my knees and threatened me. With amnesia in the original dream. Possibly with something worse tonight."

Amara skimmed a speculative finger over his wrist. "You were breathing strangely when I found you. I tried to take your pulse. You tried to punch me."

His eyes shot up. "What?"

She grinned. "I saw it coming, of course, so you missed. You hit the floor. I jumped on your back. McVey, Sarah was a small woman, no more than five foot three or four, and according to all the historical records, very slender."

"So how could she drag me to my knees?" He let his mind crawl back into the nightmare. "Annalee," he murmured, and heard Amara's comprehending "Ah."

"I was a girl in the dream," he went on. "Seven, maybe eight years old. I was hiding in the attic. Sarah pulled a dripping black blob out of a boiling pot and handed it to a man."

"Did the man have long black hair and the face of a demigod?"

Amusement stirred. "From the perspective of both man and child, Amara, he was just a guy in a cloak."

"Some people say… Uh, okay, are we leaving?"

As lightning raced through the sky, McVey stood, flexed a sore left shoulder—he probably didn't want to know the source of that injury—and extended a hand. "I'm in the mood for some raven's blood wine. If you have theories, and I'll lay odds you do, we can talk about them downstairs."

Instead of appearing rattled, she trailed a suggestive finger over his collarbone. "The wine part's an excellent idea, and the prospect of talk's intriguing, but I think I'd like something more stimulating between the first and second things."

He allowed himself a brief smile when her hand clamped his half-zipped fly, and he felt his body's instinctive reaction. "Having been trapped inside a girl's body a few minutes ago, I'm more than happy to find myself back on form." He ran his gaze over her face as the heat in his groin ramped up to painful proportions. "In fact…"

Eyes glittering, he lifted her off the floor by her hips. Her long legs twined automatically around him. With his mouth already locked on hers and need raging like thunder inside him, he found the nearest wall, pressed her to it and tossed the last of his nightmare into the storm where it belonged.

"Let me get this straight." Inside Hannah's cozy west wing living room, with a wood fire glowing in the hearth, Amara endeavored to sort through all that McVey had related. "In your dream—okay, nightmare—your name is Annalee. As Annalee, you saw Sarah give Hezekiah something black and icky, probably a magical root. After Hezekiah left, you heard her claim that brother was going to destroy brother. Meaning Hezekiah was going to destroy Ezekiel for raping and murdering Hezekiah's wife, Nola. You're saying it really was Sarah who gave Hezekiah the power to be…well, evil."

"Sarah knew Ezekiel had betrayed her love. She knew he wanted Nola for himself."

"That part's in the original legend, the one written by the Blumes. But years ago a Bellam suggested the very thing you're telling me now. That Sarah was actually the 'evil' spirit. That she caused Hezekiah to go on a killing spree. Except Nola wasn't dead, only in a state of limbo. When Hezekiah's spree ended, it was Nola who came to him as a 'good' spirit."

McVey took a long drink of wine. "A good spirit in the form of a raven."

"Raven Nola told human Hezekiah that the best she could do was transform him into a raven as well, a condition in which he would remain until someone who was fated to die succeeded in cheating death."

"Told you it was a nightmare."

"But with a slightly different twist tonight, one you sleepwalked through."

His gaze swept across the high ceiling. "Could be the surroundings. Proximity to the place where the original nightmare unfolded."

Thoughtful now, she poured him another glass of wine. "Still, McVey, everything you've said is just background information to the really fascinating part."

"That I was a girl in a former life?"

"That you were Nola's daughter in a former life. I had a dream, too, the night we stayed in the raven tamers' camp. The name Annalee came up. I was sure I'd heard it before, and it turns out I had. Annalee was Nola's daughter, born before she met Hezekiah. You were Annalee."

"Only if you believe in reincarnation, Red. Which I don't."

"Which you don't want to." She curled her legs under

his black T-shirt, then, unable to resist, leaned in to whisper an amused, "Makes you a Bellam, you know."

He poured more of the wine into her glass. "I guess it also makes us kissing cousins."

"Fifty or sixty times removed. Tell me, have you ever had the urge to cast a spell?"

"Or ride a broomstick?"

"No male Bellam ever rode a broomstick, McVey. I doubt if any of them even knew what one looked like."

"Apparently, I'm more enlightened. I swept the floors in my father's antiques shop as a kid."

"I love antiques—" Her head came up as something slammed against the side of the house. "Well, wow. If that whatever-it-was was wind driven, Bellam Bridge might not even be in the state of Maine tomorrow. Which could be good or bad, depending on Willy Sparks's present location—and why on earth did I bring that up?"

McVey shifted so they were both facing the fire. Resting an arm across her shoulders, he played with her hair. "Talk more about Sarah."

"What? Oh." She pushed fear aside and gave his leg a smiling pat. "That's your story. You said Sarah said she wanted both Hezekiah and Ezekiel destroyed so she and her unborn child—Ezekiel's child, obviously—could inherit Hezekiah's vast estate. Money, land, homes, et cetera."

He grinned. "Give the woman credit, it was an ambitious plan."

"Yes, and only two Blumes and a Bellam had to die for her to achieve it. Oh, and I forgot, all the townspeople who followed Ezekiel into the woods and helped him 'murder' Nola."

"Ambition isn't always pretty, Red."

"Jimmy Sparks is an ambitious man."

"So was I once, in what I thought at the time was a more positive way." McVey took a drink of the bloodred wine. "Life can screw you. Lines are irrelevant. Good, bad, pick a side, stand back and watch the mighty fall."

She regarded his profile. "I'd call that an extremely cryptic remark. I hope you're going to elaborate and not force me to draw my own conclusions."

He linked the fingers of his left hand with her right. "Let's just say my last bust as a city cop proved to me that once in a while the so-called good guys go bad. Unfortunately, if their connections within the department are important enough and reach high enough, Internal Affairs will turn a blind eye and the dirty deeds will get shunted to the investigative morgue."

"Causing at least one good cop to go looking for something better. Somewhere better. In this case, a spooky little town on the coast of Maine."

McVey examined the wine bottle. "We're down to the dregs, Red, and I'm not feeling a single adverse effect. You?"

"No, but then I hit my head when we made love in the shower, so I can attribute any dizziness I might be experiencing to that."

"I'm the one who got whacked by the showerhead." When Amara laughed, he set the bottle aside and pulled her onto his lap. "If you're dizzy, what you need is exercise."

"From a medical standpoint, I have to tell you, that's really bad advice. However…" Eyes dancing, she hooked her arms around his neck and wriggled until he went hard. "Seeing as I know what you're doing and what you want, all I can say is—"

The rest of the sentence stuck in her throat as lightning

flickered and her eyes, now facing the living room window, picked up a movement. For a split second she saw someone in the driveway.

Someone wearing rain gear and carrying a rifle.

Chapter Fifteen

"You coulda shouted, McVey." Clearly annoyed, Brigham stripped off his muddy raincoat and dumped it on the porch. "Come at me like a battering ram and I'm gonna batter right back."

McVey took the bag of frozen garden peas Amara handed him and pressed it to the side of the knee Brigham had injured during their brief skirmish. She plunked a similar bag of lima beans on Brigham's head and told herself this ridiculous comedy of errors wasn't funny. It could have been Willy Sparks or even Hannah's killer sneaking around the perimeter of the manor instead of her raven tamer cousin.

"You helped Rune," Brigham grumbled, "so I figured I'd help you."

"Next time, mention it," McVey said through his teeth. "I'm too young to be thinking about having reconstructive surgery on my knee."

As she rooted through the cupboards, Amara shook her head. "You're never too young, McVey. I've reconstructed feet, ankles, knees, hips—the list goes on and up—for people a lot younger than you." She located a bottle of amber liquid and held it up for Brigham to see. "Is this raven tamer whiskey?"

"I don't know. My head hurts worse when I open my eyes. If there's no label, it's ours, and gimme."

She placed it in the middle of the kitchen table within easy reach of both men. "You can share the bottle or wait until I wash some of the glasses Hannah left piled in the sink. I'll go out on a limb here and speculate that dish washing wasn't one of her favorite chores."

Brigham shot McVey a glare. "I can handle a dirty glass."

"As a medical practitioner, I'm forced to say, yuck."

McVey worked up a faint smile. "Is that doctor talk for 'it's an unhealthy practice'?"

"No, it's woman talk for 'it's gross.' There's black gunk hardened on the bottom of every mug, it'll take a week's worth of soaking to soften whatever she burned onto this casserole dish and the red stains in the wineglasses are probably permanent by now.... Why didn't you tell us you planned to stick around, Brigham?"

The big man shrugged. "Didn't know it myself until we started moving out. Then it came to me. Too many people are dead who shouldn't be. Would a hit man leave a trail of bodies like this?"

McVey reached for the bottle, took a long drink and shot it across the table. "Depends on the hit man. In Willy Sparks's case, I'd say it's unlikely."

The lights, which had held to this point, began to wink out as Amara filled the sink with hot water. "I still can't think why anyone would want Hannah dead. We assume Westor witnessed something in the alley at the Red Eye. Possibly ditto for Mina, but..."

"Is she the tourist I heard about?" Brigham asked.

McVey shifted the frozen peas to the other side of his knee. "One more piece of our ever-expanding puzzle."

Amara glanced up as the lights fluttered again. "It

crossed my mind that Mina and Westor were…you know, together."

McVey nodded. "You could be right. Jake said he found sleeping bags—plural—in an empty apartment in Yolanda's building. I'll check it out when we get back."

"If we get back." Twitching off a chill, Amara plunged her hands into the hot, soapy water.

Westor's and Mina's deaths disturbed her, but Hannah's completely baffled her. She'd been a harmless eccentric—a hermit with a bad leg and really nothing a thief might want.

Amara wondered if her mental state had been deteriorating without anyone realizing it. She could have had too much to drink, wandered into the manor's central core and bumped into a homicidal hobo.

"Right," she said under her breath. "A hobo who took the murder weapon with him when he left, because…" Like the question, her theory sputtered out.

Behind her, McVey and Brigham continued to bait each other while the overhead lights surged and faded. They winked off completely, but popped on again as she put the last glass in the drain rack.

Still wearing his frozen vegetable hat, Brigham took a swig of whiskey and fished an iPod out of his shirt pocket. "I'll take first watch, Amara, if you and McVey have something you'd rather be doing upstairs."

She regarded him through mistrustful eyes. "You weren't spying on us earlier, were you?"

"Only in my lurid imagination." He made a sideways motion. "I'll camp out in the living room."

She watched him lumber away, grunting out an old Johnny Cash song.

McVey went to take stock of the yard through the kitchen window. "I don't see Sparks braving a storm like this on the off chance he might be able to get to you. Not sure about our mysterious other."

From spectacular sex to abject terror—she'd run the gamut tonight, Amara decided. And dawn was still several hours away.

"You missed a spot, Red." McVey surprised her by coming up from behind and tugging on her hair. "Don't get tangled up in all the loose threads. You'll only freak yourself out."

She rubbed at a smear on the rim of a wineglass. "I've been freaked out since I walked onto a hotel balcony in the Vieux Carré and watched Jimmy Sparks put a bullet in a woman's chest. She took one step, McVey, and dropped like a stone. It happened in a back alley on a night almost exactly like this. Sparks didn't check to see if there might be witnesses. He just stormed into the alley and shot her."

"Jimmy Sparks is famous for his volatile temper."

"His lawyers claimed it was a drug-induced homicide. He takes a number of meds, all of which are strong, but none of which, even in combination, would drive a rational man to commit murder. The victim was a call girl. She tried to roll him. He took exception. That's not good when the John in question is known to fly into violent rages without warning."

"What were you doing on a hotel balcony in the Vieux Carré?"

"I was visiting a patient, doing a follow-up to a surgery I'd performed. She wasn't a friend exactly, but I liked her and I wanted to make sure she was happy with the results."

"She being Georgia Arnault, former registered nurse and mother of six. Lives in a small town in the bayou. Her cousin works at the same hospital as you."

"You've done your homework." Amara arched a brow. "Should I be impressed or flattered?"

"Fact-finding's easy when you're a cop. In this case, the deeper I dug, the more I learned."

"And didn't like."

"It's hard to like a police officer who'd abuse his badge the way your patient's boyfriend did over—what was it?—a ten-year period."

"Twelve. Every cop on the force in the town where they lived knew he was beating her. That's five men who refused to see or act. Georgia said it was a solidarity thing, good old boys sticking together. I say all of them, and her so-called boyfriend most especially, should be subject to the removal of certain body parts."

"I wouldn't argue with that." McVey tucked a strand of hair behind her ear. "You reconstructed Georgia's face—nose, cheekbones, chin—and erased as much of the damage as you could."

"She'd been working on the emotional side of things, seeing a psychologist in New Orleans, which was why she was in a hotel the night of the murder. We were both on the balcony at one point. But Georgia's afraid of thunderstorms, and the storm that night was wild.... What are you doing?" Amusement swam up into her eyes when he scooped her off her feet. "I saw that knee of yours, McVey. You can't possibly carry me all the way upstairs and down the hall without experiencing tremendous pain."

Hiking her higher, he caught her mouth for a mind-numbing kiss that stripped away her breath and her mild protest. "I won't be experiencing any pain, Amara. Not until tomorrow anyway."

She repositioned herself in his arms and used her teeth on his earlobe. When his eyes glazed, she whispered a teasing, "Wanna bet?"

Owing to the fact that Bellam Bridge appeared to be standing more out of stubbornness than any true structural support, Brigham reluctantly showed them an alternate route off the mountain.

"Mention this to anyone," he warned, "and not only will you be 'uncommon' faster than you can blink, but you'll also find yourselves being watched by ravens every night."

Clinging to the base of a sapling and preparing to jump off a six-foot ledge into a puddle of mud, Amara didn't ask the obvious question. She merely reminded herself that he was on her side and not trying to help Willy Sparks achieve his murderous goal.

It took them more than ninety minutes to access the main road. They backtracked for another twenty to McVey's truck, then squeezed into the cab for the remainder of the bumpy trip.

Fanning her face with a clipboard from the dash, she pushed on her cousin's massive leg. "I'm not six inches wide, Brigham."

"You want me to ride in the back like a dog?"

"No, I want you to tell me what the deal is with staring ravens."

He grinned at her cross tone. "Hell, that's Legend 101, Amara. Feathers delivered to doorsteps by a raven mean death. Ravens that sit and watch are doing it on someone else's behalf."

"Someone good or someone evil?"

He bared his teeth in a menacing smile. "That's for you to figure out."

She frowned up at him. "Are you trying to scare me because I landed on your foot when I jumped from that big boulder earlier?"

McVey, who'd remained silent until now, chuckled. "More likely he's cranky because he's hungover and Hannah's coffee tasted like crap. Ravens fly, land and occasionally stare, Amara. So do crows and no one thinks twice about it."

Brigham snorted out a laugh. "Unless the people those crows are`staring at live in Bodega Bay and they've watched *The Birds* one too many times." At Amara's exasperated look, he shrugged a beefy shoulder. "Just saying."

"You know as well as I do that ravens have a stigma attached to them. When he was a raven, Hezekiah's action—leaving feathers on doors—portended death, but didn't actively cause it. He was a sort of middleman."

"Middle raven," McVey said.

Because she knew he was trying not to grin, she jabbed an elbow into his ribs before reaching for his ringing phone.

"We're driving, Jake," she said. "On a road that requires skill and concentration. I'm putting you on speaker."

The deputy opened with an irritable, "There's a bunch of raven tamers wandering around the Hollow, McVey. People keep giving them the thumbs-up sign. Can I arrest them on the grounds that they're gonna get half the town tanked tonight on their illegal hooch?"

"It's not hooch," Brigham shouted over Amara. "It's frigging superior whiskey and wine that goes down like honey."

McVey's lips quirked. "Been a while since you've drunk your own wine, I think."

On the other end of the phone, Jake growled out a terse, "Tell me you're not giving a raven tamer a police escort into town, McVey. Some old crone tried to tell me you were tight with them now and I should mind my own if I want to go on being a deputy, but I figured she was drunk on her own stuff and hallucinating."

McVey braked for a deer. "Leave the raven tamers alone,

Jake. Their parade kick-starts the festivities. It's tradition. What's the real problem?"

"I got six positives from the DMV for the name Mina Shell. Two of them might be her. I did background checks. North Carolina Mina has brown hair, not blond, and I can't see her eyes very well. She's twenty-eight and works in a bank. Nashville, Tennessee, Mina is a dental hygienist and looks thinner than corpse Mina, but weight changes and these printouts are lousy anyway."

"Did you run our Mina's fingerprints?"

"Er, yeah. Just."

McVey swore softly. "Get a clear set, Jake. Is the sheriff still there?"

"He left two hours ago. Something about a domestic hostage-taking five blocks from his office."

"Send the victim's fingerprints off to the county lab before I get back. You've got about thirty minutes....Shut up, Brigham," he said in the same uninflected tone after disconnecting. "Deputies are as hard to come by as police chiefs in these parts."

Amara sighed. "It wouldn't matter how good either of them was if I'd gone into hiding in New York instead of here."

"We've been down this road more than once, Red." McVey eased through a deep puddle. "Hannah's not dead because of you."

Inasmuch as she could, Amara folded her arms. "Westor is. And probably Mina."

"Westor came here wanting revenge on me."

Brigham bumped Amara's leg with his. "We in the raven tamer community call a death like his poetic justice."

"What do you call Mina's death?"

"Would you feel better if everyone hereabouts just said

to hell with it and told this Willy Sparks person where to find you?" Brigham demanded.

She worked herself around to glare. Then an idea occurred and her animosity dissolved. "Actually, that could work."

Brigham glanced at McVey, shrugged. "You had to figure. Descended from Sarah Bellam and Ezekiel Blume, the crazy was bound to pop out at some point."

Because any other movement required too much effort, Amara kicked the big man's foot. "I'm talking about setting Willy Sparks up, not running through town with a target painted on my chest. Have you ever done that, McVey? Drawn a murderer out using bait?"

"Twice."

"Did it work?"

"We used a ringer the first time. He got shot in the shoulder and the leg. The second time, circumstances forced us to go with the intended victim. He survived but three officers were hit. One died." A brow went up. "Answer your question?"

Unfortunately, yes. But that didn't mean she had to like it or to close her mind completely to the possibility. This was small-town Maine, not Chicago or New York. They might be able to minimize the risks in a more constricted environment.

Or more people might die and Willy Sparks would slip away into the night.

Guilt gnawed at her for the remainder of the drive.

They dropped Brigham off at a service station half a mile from her uncle's motel, which was apparently where the raven tamers would be staying during the Night of the Raven festival. They stayed, they paid. When it came to money, Lazarus Blume seldom missed a trick.

While Brigham leaned in the window of McVey's truck for a final chat, Amara bought coffee and used the station's restroom.

Locked in, she stared at her reflection in the hazy mirror.

She could leave right now, today, and not tell a soul. She only had to let McVey become embroiled, then she could borrow her uncle's truck and disappear. Force Willy Sparks to come after her.

Give Willy Sparks a perfect opportunity to kill her. "Because, face it, Red," she mocked her reflection. "He'll do it before the day runs out. Everyone who's dead will still be dead, and like McVey said, he'll simply fly off to a tropical destination and wait for new orders." She huffed out her frustration. "I hate cop logic."

She saw McVey heading toward the building as she stepped back outside. "I was thinking…" She frowned when he grabbed her hand and pulled. "What is it?"

"Jake called."

She had to trot to keep up. "Obviously with bad news." Her blood turned to ice and she clutched his arm with her free hand. "Please tell me no one else is dead."

"No one else is dead, Amara." He didn't wait for her to climb up, but caught her by the waist and set her in his truck.

"What's going on?" she demanded again. "What did Jake say?"

For the first time since they'd met, McVey turned on the flashing lights and siren. "He tried to take Mina Shell's fingerprints. He couldn't get anything."

She opened her mouth, considered and closed it again. "That's impossible. Everyone has fingerprints. Unless Mina…"

"Yeah." He tossed her a look rich in meaning. "Unless Mina."

Amara stared at her own fingertips. "Are you saying she deliberately removed them? Well, yes, you are. But—ouch."

"Big ouch. Done for a big reason."

"She didn't want to be identified."

"Exactly." A grim smile appeared. "All we have to do is figure out why."

AMARA DISLIKED EXAMINING CORPSES. She actively hated touching them. But she had to see Mina's fingers for herself.

"I'm not a complete moron," Jake called across the back room at the station house. "I know how to take prints. Another hour and it would have been out of our hands. Mina Shell and Westor Hall are scheduled for transfer to the county morgue at 1:00 p.m."

Amara heard him, but only as a curious buzz in the background. "Why do I find this so incredibly creepy?" she wondered aloud.

"No idea." Jake inched cautiously closer. "I find the idea of raven tamers way creepier."

"Only because you're afraid of them."

"Isn't everyone? They're freaking lawbreakers who make themselves seem mysterious by living in the north woods and selling booze local crime labs can't analyze."

"Really?" She laid Mina's hand down but didn't rezip the body bag. "Maybe they incorporate some of Sarah's roots and powders into the mix."

"You're talking, lady, but I'm not hearing… Aw, crap sakes, Amara." Jake jerked back in revulsion when she pulled the flap down farther. "I don't wanna look at a naked dead woman."

"Neither do I, but I saw the photos you showed McVey. She has tattoos."

"A leaf, a splat and a heart with initials inside it. Who cares?"

Amara regarded the red heart over Mina's left breast. "*WS,* Jake." She raised speculative brows. "Willy Sparks, maybe?"

"You mean the guy McVey said is after you? You think she had his initials tattooed on her chest? You think she came here with a hit man?"

The clinic door opened and closed. Amara recognized McVey's long stride, but she didn't remove her gaze from the dead woman.

Jake stabbed a finger. "Amara thinks Mina Shell came to town with that hit man you've been looking for. Is she North Carolina Mina or Tennessee Mina, McVey?"

"Neither."

Amara examined the tattoo on Mina's hip. "That's a spark, isn't it?"

"Be my guess," McVey said.

"And the leaf on her shoulder. Some kind of poisonous plant?"

"Go with hemlock. I'll explain why later."

"Okay, I take it back." Jake stepped away, palms up. "She's as creepy as the raven tamers."

"Mina…" Amara let the name roll off her tongue.

"You're almost there, Red."

Something cold and slippery twisted in her stomach.

"Excuse me, people, but am I missing something?"

"*WS,* Jake." Amara said softly. "I'm willing to bet Mina's full name is Wilhelmina. Meaning Mina Shell is really Willy Sparks."

Chapter Sixteen

"What would you have done, McVey, if Mina Shell, aka Willy Sparks, hadn't brought along a passport in her real name?" Pacing her grandmother's kitchen, Amara shook her still-tingling fingers. "Would you have sent a picture of her corpse to Jimmy and had the prison guards watch to see how he reacted?"

McVey straddled a hard chair. "It's been done before. But thanks to the fact that she stashed her shoulder bag at the bottom of one of the sleeping bags in the apartment Westor was using as a flophouse, not a necessary tactic. You were right, by the way, about Willy and Westor."

"They must have walked into the alley together and at the worst possible moment—for them anyway." She ticked a finger. "But back to Willy. Could you have identified her without her passport?"

"Passport and tattoos aside, Red, Willy Sparks had a scar where her appendix was removed."

"Saw that. It's at least ten years old…. Ah, right. Hospitals keep computer records."

"And more criminals than you might expect use their real names for surgeries. On top of that, at eighteen years of age, most girls aren't thinking they'll become hit men for their uncles after college."

"I don't know, McVey. I had my career path firmly in mind at eighteen."

"Willy's appendectomy was an emergency surgery. No time for fake IDs."

She smiled. "I love a thorough man."

"It never hurts to double-check. As for her picture, I might have sent it to Jimmy Sparks—if my motive had been anything other than pure spite."

"Probably just as well. Lieutenant Michaels said Jimmy's health has been declining steadily since his incarceration. Seeing his niece in a morgue might be too traumatic for him to handle." Amara's brows came together. "Am I feeling sorry for a man who murdered a call girl and three people I knew in cold blood?"

"You're a doctor, you're allowed to be compassionate." A smile touched McVey's lips. He caught her hand in passing. "Makes you better than him."

"Right. Good." She regarded their joined hands. "Why am I still spooked?"

"Because there are significant questions that still need to be answered."

"Like who killed Willy Sparks and Westor Hall? Or did they kill each other?" She considered for a moment. "Maybe Westor saw Willy tossing a Molotov cocktail into the Red Eye. Willy pulled a gun on him, he pulled one on her and they both pulled the trigger."

"It's a tidy theory, Red."

"I'm getting more invalid than tidy. Why?"

"The only weapons Westor ever used were knives—specifically his own—and rifles. Willy was shot with a Luger."

"And Westor?"

"Same weapon."

Frustration swept in. "So what now? With Willy Sparks

out of the picture, am I safe from Uncle Jimmy? Or will he have a contingency plan I should worry about?"

"I doubt if he knows about Willy yet, unless they had some prearranged check-in that she missed."

"Meaning my extended family and I are safe?"

"From Jimmy Sparks, probably, for the moment. From our mysterious other? That depends on his or her motive, which unfortunately we haven't established."

Amara drilled the fingers of her other hand into her temple. "My head feels like a centrifuge. You're telling me Willy and Westor were both shot with a Luger in the alley outside the Red Eye the night the bar was firebombed. Are we assuming the mysterious other who killed Hannah is the firebomber, or are we going with a different person?"

McVey ran his thumb over the back of her hand. "For no reason beyond gut instinct, I'm going with the mysterious other as both Hannah's murderer and the firebomber."

"Two killers, then, and one of them, Willy Sparks, is gone. I swear my brain's going to implode."

Standing, he tipped her chin up and kissed her until the implosion became a fiery blast of heat.

"Well, good on you, Chief," she managed to say when her mouth was her own again. "Our entire conversation flashed briefly before my eyes, then vanished in a puff of smoke." Setting her tongue on her upper lip, she snagged his waistband and backed toward the rear staircase. "Rumor has it the raven tamers will be doing some preparade publicity in and around the Hollow after sunset. You probably shouldn't miss that, given Jake's weirdly obsessive desire to lock them up and toss the key. Having said that, however, sunset is still hours away." She mounted a step, tugged him closer and bit his lip. "You've been pulling double shifts." Both hands fisted in his hair. "And I want sex." She kissed him long and hard. "Right here, right now. With you."

His dark eyes gleamed in the shadowed light of the stairwell. "Got you covered there, Red."

Lifting her off her feet, he spun her back to the wall and took her as she'd hoped right where they stood.

MAKING LOVE WITH Amara was the lone bright spot in an otherwise problem-filled day. Unless he counted the discovery of Willy Sparks's purse, which had contained five hundred dollars in cash, a bank card, her passport, keys to a Jeep—he'd sent one of the Harden twins out to search for that—a pressed powder compact and four tubes of bubblegum–pink lipstick.

"I bought right into her story." Amara flicked through the lookalike tubes. "Do you think Westor and Willy had already met the day Westor threatened me in the pharmacy?"

"I don't think Westor had been in the Hollow long at that point, and we know Willy was a new arrival, so I'd say probably not. You said he grabbed her, too?"

"By the scruff of the neck."

"Some people find a dangerous meeting sexually stimulating."

She laughed. "No comment." Then she raised a speculative brow. "Westor couldn't have known he was having sex with a hit man, could he?"

"Not a chance. One, Willy wouldn't have told him, and two, he'd have pissed himself if she had. It's not the kind of knowledge a person wants to possess. You know, you die. Westor didn't want to die."

"But he did die."

"Not at the hands of Willy Sparks."

"And the wheels spin in place yet again." She shook it

off. "I'm going to balance my mind and spend a few hours at the clinic."

McVey frowned. "Jake broke a tooth at lunch, Amara. I sent him to Bangor to have it fixed."

"Now, there, you see? Every cloud does have a silver lining."

He slid a hand along her bare arm. "I don't want you at the clinic alone."

She motioned toward the door. "Willy's gone, McVey. She and Westor left four hours ago. Even if corpses could do the zombie thing and arise, she'd have to hitchhike back here to do whatever it was she'd planned to do to me." Sidetracked by her own statement, Amara hesitated. "What do you think she planned to do?"

McVey pushed off from the front desk where he'd paused to perch. "Doesn't matter what she planned. It only matters that she didn't succeed."

Amara released a ragged breath. "I guess I love cop logic after all. Don't ask." She kissed his cheek. "I'll let Brigham play guard dog. He's been doing it since we got to town anyway."

"Being common has its advantages."

"Apparently." She kissed him again. "Catch you at the preparade party, Chief. I've got notes to compare with the local midwife on Megan's pregnancy."

And he had two towns to police. Towns that were filling up fast with a mix of watchers and participants. He had no idea where the majority of them might be staying, although when fully open and occupied, word had it Blume House could accommodate a large number of guests. Directly below the house stood the also-large Ravenspell campsite. And farther afield, serious tenters could choose from a number of north woods clearings.

Satisfied that Amara would be safe—he'd spoken to Brigham earlier—McVey turned his mind to other matters.

Lazarus Blume had texted him an hour ago. He wanted Hannah's personal effects brought to the motel as soon as possible. Tomorrow would have to do. In the meantime, McVey thought, if he could eke out an hour or two, Hannah's Blume's death required a great deal more investigation.

Forensics had discovered a substantial amount of alcohol in her system, but no poisons or painkillers. Factor in the impossible positioning of her body and, any way he approached it, her death read like a homicide.

So. Had Luger-man killed her, or were they dealing with a pair of murderers?

Lieutenant Michaels's captain had contacted him that morning. Michaels had been poisoned with a derivative of the hemlock plant called conium, a toxin usually introduced to its victim through some form of liquid. That probably explained the hemlock-leaf tattoo on Willy Sparks's body. One swallow of whatever she'd poisoned and the lieutenant had been a dead man. Westor and Willy, on the other hand, had died in a far more blatant fashion.

The station phone rang as he was pulling up files on Westor and the Sparks family. He glanced at the computer screen and clamped down an urge to swear.

"Hey there, handsome," a familiar voice cooed.

"No, you can't have a last-minute license to sell liquor in the street, Yolanda."

There was a trace of venom under her petulant response. "Well, that's just mean, isn't it? You know I can't miss the Night. I was telling Uncle Lazarus earlier how easy it would be to do a tent with benches and tables. Like an Oktoberfest. I have stock. The Red Eye's cellar didn't burn."

He was tempted to cave but... "Okay, here's the deal.

Email me a plan that works, and I'll think about issuing a license for tomorrow night."

Her already high-pitched voice rose. "By tomorrow, the raven tamers will have over half the town buying their stuff, and the rest will defect to Two Toes Joe's in the Cove. I can't afford to lose my regulars."

McVey tapped a few computer keys, saw nothing of interest and rocked his head from side to side to ease the building tension. "Look, you didn't hear this from me, but why don't you talk to Brigham about selling raven's blood in your rebuilt Red Eye? Come to an agreement, and the tamers might let you have a barrel or two for your temporary street digs. That should entice your regulars back. Tomorrow."

"I don't like raven tamers, McVey. My brother says a single bottle of their whiskey could blow out the side of Bellam Mountain more effectively than nitro. He figures if the crazy person who firebombed me out of business had been smart, he'd have used it in his Molotov cocktails. Who needs gasoline when you've got raven tamer whiskey?"

"Send me a plan."

"McVey…"

Damn her. The wounded tone struck its mark. Unfortunately he wasn't in the mood to be guilt-tripped. "Really busy here, Yolanda."

"She won't stay, you know. She wouldn't make you happy if she did. And that's a big 'if' considering a baddie like Jimmy Sparks wants her dead." The venom bled back in. "My bar's gone because of her."

"Your bar's gone because someone—not Amara—rigged explosives to blow inside and tossed firebombs through a couple of windows. Talk to Brigham about the raven's blood. Sorry, but I've got work."

He cut her off midprotest, called himself a bastard for his lack of sympathy and turned back to Jimmy Sparks's police file.

He spent forty minutes with the reports, but knew his viewing time was up when the remaining Harden twin stuck his head in the door.

"Got a problem brewing, Chief."

"Blume, Bellam or raven tamer?"

"Yes. And all six of them are boiling mad."

An unanticipated spark ignited in McVey's belly and spread quickly to his eyes. Oh, yeah, here it was. This was why he'd come to Maine. Where else on the globe could a legend about a transformed raven clash with a legend about a mad witch and cause people to come to blows? Only in the place where those legends had been born.

The place where the person he'd been long ago had been born.

AMARA WORKED AT the clinic until Brigham insisted he needed food.

"We've got a caravan, a truck and a couple of jazzed-up wagons parked along Main and in front of the square. Marta's big on sausages, root vegetables and herbs roasted in their own juices. Makes the street smell like heaven." He shrugged. "We mostly do it for the tourists and the show. I planted a garden once, and everything I grew turned black."

"Vegetable gardens do very well everywhere else in the north woods." Amara grinned. "Maybe Sarah cursed the soil on and around Bellam Mountain." Movement at her feet distracted her. "Ground fog. Very cool. Looks like snakes. Did you order this as part of your pre-Night publicity?"

"No, but if you tell Marta you conjured it, could be she'll cut you in on a share of the profits."

"Which I in turn could funnel into the Hollow's so-called medical clinic."

Brigham sniffed the air. "Roasted yams and beef stew. Man, I'm starved. Never thought I'd say that after seeing a man with some kind of foot fungus."

She laughed. "Do you know if McVey's here or in the Cove?"

"He drove to the Cove to check in at his badly neglected office."

"Wonderful. More guilt on me."

The shoulder knock Brigham gave her almost sent her into the side of a painted wagon. "Don't sweat it, Amara. Cove people being mostly Blumes are used to not having a police chief around. Trouble tends to unfold more in the Hollow, where mostly Bellams live."

"At the risk of sounding contentious, you raven tamers—mostly Blumes—currently reside on Bellam Mountain and are planning to line your collective Blume pockets with a substantial amount of Bellam money during the festival."

"Pick, pick, pick." Brigham jerked a thumb. "I'm getting some of my cousin Imogene's stew. Stay where the light's good."

She'd have to go to Bangor to do that, Amara reflected, because neither the Cove nor the Hollow boasted well-lit streets.

The scent of fresh buttermilk biscuits drew her toward a red-and-black caravan with a collection of animated ravens on the top. She was marveling at the combination of artistry and engineering when her phone went off.

Her first thought was McVey. Her second was *Damn*. But she sucked it up and summoned a pleasant "Hi, Uncle Lazarus. Sorry, I got sidetracked. I'll bring Hannah's things to the motel as soon as McVey gets back from the Cove."

Raspy breathing on the other end had her raising wary eyes. "Uncle Lazarus?"

"Amara…" He wheezed out her name. "Not sure… Might be my heart. I…took a pill."

She spotted McVey climbing out of his truck and jogged across the street toward him. "When did you take it, Uncle?"

"Five, ten minutes ago." He sounded painfully short of breath, which might or might not be due to his heart condition.

"Breathe as evenly as you can and try not to move. Where's R.J.?"

"Went to the Cove… Still there."

Amara waved McVey back to his truck.

"Problem?" he asked.

She covered the phone. "It's Uncle Lazarus. He might be having a heart attack."

"Motel?"

She nodded, returned her attention to her uncle. "I need you to stay on the line. Don't exert, just relax and breathe. Are you sitting down?"

"Yes."

"Good. Now stay where you are, no extraneous movement."

"No extran…" He tapered off.

McVey spoke to one of the Hardens. The young deputy nodded and took off running. Tossing her medical bag onto the seat, Amara climbed into the truck. "Uncle Lazarus, do you have R.J.'s cell number?"

Her uncle's voice came back reed thin. "Not memorized… Speed dial."

"Okay. McVey's here. We're on our way. We'll be there in…"

"Fifteen minutes."

McVey flipped on the siren and flashers to clear a path through town. Amara put her uncle on hold and punched 9-1-1.

What had been ground fog in the Hollow thickened and crawled higher as they wound their way toward the motel. Filmy finger clouds stretched across the face of a nearly full moon. If the leaves hadn't been new and green, May could have passed for October—although why she was thinking ridiculous thoughts like that when her uncle might be having a massive coronary, she couldn't imagine.

"He didn't mention pain," she said to herself. "But I can hear he's short of breath." She made a seesaw motion with her head. "Happens. Not all the symptoms all the time." She raised her voice. "What's the usual response for the paramedics, McVey?"

"As much as thirty minutes. If we take the old logging road, we can shave five off our time."

"It would help."

For the life of her Amara had no idea how any vehicle could navigate ruts large enough to swallow a full-grown man. But somehow McVey pulled it off. Several terrifying pitches later she realized that they were only a mile or so from the motel.

"Uncle Lazarus?" she said into her phone.

He didn't respond.

When the skin on her neck prickled, she glanced around. "Something's wrong. Do you feel it?"

"Define *it,* Amara."

"I don't mean Uncle Lazarus. Or not just him. I was examining a woman's breast this afternoon and suddenly my mind wandered off. That never happens. I'm not sure where it was trying to go, but it never got there. Is that stress or is the general weirdness of the area getting to me?"

"You lost me at 'woman's breast.' And I'm still coming to terms with the general weirdness of the area."

"That's not exactly… Oh, good, we're here." She took a moment to regard the collection of wagons and caravans parked every which way around the motel. "Whoa, raven tamers. Go big or go home."

A single light burning in her uncle's room brought her back. Grabbing her medical bag, she hopped out and ran for the door.

She had her hand on the knob. Then suddenly she didn't. The ground under her feet vanished. So did the air in her lungs as she landed on top of McVey in a patch of gravel, dirt and weeds.

She couldn't speak, literally could not get enough breath into her lungs to make a sound. But McVey covered her mouth anyway and rolled them both into a crouch.

"There's someone inside."

The clutch of stars that had erupted in Amara's head faded. Her brain settled sufficiently for her to understand they weren't alone. Not them, and not her uncle.

She twisted on McVey's wrist.

"No sound," he cautioned, releasing her.

She drank in the cool night air. Her knees wanted to buckle and her chest felt as if Brigham's foot was lodged in it, but at least the ground was beginning to steady.

"Did you see Uncle Lazarus?"

"He's slumped over the table." As he spoke, McVey drew his Glock. "Backup's in my left boot. Get it, stay low and stay behind me."

Who was inside? The question echoed in Amara's head. It had to be the person who'd killed Hannah, didn't it?

At the edge of the window, McVey aimed his gun skyward.

They heard it a second later—a protracted creak behind the motel. A creak, followed by a slam, followed by an engine roaring to life.

With his gun still angled up, McVey shouted, "Get inside. Doors locked, shades down. Minimum light." He tossed her his keys. "Use my truck to drive him out if you have to."

"I— Yes, okay." She ran, spun. "Be careful." Already at the door, she shook off her frustration. "Part man, part Merlin."

Naturally the door jammed when she tried the knob. To her relief, one hard shoulder bump and it sprang open.

"Uncle Lazarus?" Shoving the dead bolt in place, Amara yanked the shade down but left the light in the kitchenette burning. She needed something to see by.

She set McVey's gun and her cell phone aside, went to her knees and checked her uncle's neck for a pulse. Thready and rapid, she realized. Too rapid.

With her left hand she unzipped her bag and pulled out her stethoscope. Pushing away a glass of milk, she placed the chest piece over his heart and listened.

His heart was definitely beating too fast, yet there was no sign of ventricular fibrillation. "Hmm." Removing the earpieces, she lifted one of her uncle's eyelids, sat back and thought for a moment.

Her uncle suffered from arrhythmia—an irregular heartbeat—for which he took medication. Yes, his heartbeat was wrong, and he'd sounded extremely short of breath on the phone, but he'd taken a pill to combat the condition.

"Need to see your meds," she declared.

She made a point of switching off the light in the kitchenette before turning on the much stingier one in the bathroom.

"You could be a little less frugal where your own comfort is concerned," she muttered and, knowing exactly what her uncle would say to that, let a faint smile cross her lips.

Her brief amusement lasted until she opened the medicine cabinet. One look inside had a scream leaping into her throat and her vision starting to blur.

Chapter Seventeen

The engine of Lazarus Blume's 1954 Dodge continued to roar long after McVey reached the corner of the motel. Although the ass end of the truck was pointed toward him, he had no sight line through the rear window.

He knew a ruse when he saw one. He also knew movement when he spotted it, and he saw someone dart around the front of the truck into the shadows of the motel. It wouldn't have been a problem if there hadn't been twenty raven tamer vehicles parked at cross purposes directly in front of him.

With Lazarus's truck belching exhaust and tendrils of fog winding around everything in sight, McVey stayed low and eased forward.

He caught sight of the figure thirty feet ahead. Bent slightly at the waist, it crept along the side of a caravan. It seemed to be searching for something.

Or someone, McVey reflected darkly.

Cutting the guy off was easy enough. He slipped between two trucks, skirted a tall wagon and waited until the man tried to sneak past the hitch. When he did, McVey met him gun first with the barrel aimed at his head.

"Hey, R.J.," he said softly. "Why the military stealth?"

Lazarus's nephew froze, raised his hands. "Don't be

getting trigger-happy, McVey. I have no quarrel with you. I just got here myself."

"In your uncle's truck?"

"Hell no, in my own. It's parked out front of cabin ten. I hightailed it back here when I heard Lazarus's old Dodge start up. He's not supposed to drive at night."

"He's not in the cab," McVey told him. He made a quick but thorough sweep of the shadows. "No one is. The truck's a diversion. I thought you were the perp."

"What I am," R.J. countered, "is confused. I saw right away there was no one in the truck, yet all the lights are on and the engine's racing. Lazarus babies that engine. He won't let anyone but him behind the wheel. So like I said—confused. Can I drop my hands now?"

"Be my guest." McVey looked from wagon to truck to caravan. "Have you seen anyone in the past few minutes?"

"Haven't seen anyone at all. That's the problem. But I know this. Trucks don't start themselves, and you wouldn't be sneaking around here with a gun if they did. What the crap's going on?"

"I'll let you know when I find out."

He spotted it a split second too late. By the time the quiet thwack that made R.J.'s eyes widen registered, the cane was less than a foot from his head.

He had no time to prevent or even deflect the blow.

But he glimpsed color and had enough time to curse himself for not twigging to the deception sooner. Raven tamer whiskey got people drunk quickly, and it could do a lot more than burn holes in stomach linings. A hell of a lot more.

As pain shot through his skull, however, it wasn't whiskey McVey thought about—it was Amara. She was inside her uncle's motel room. Safe from Willy Sparks, but not from a much closer killer. A killer whose motives and methods mimicked those of a long-dead, frighteningly mad witch.

"UNCLE LAZARUS!" AMARA gave him a desperate shake. Her eyes darted around the room. "Wake up! Please, I need you to wake up so we can get out of— Damn! Damn, damn!"

She jerked upright, her gaze glued to the floor.

"Uncle Laz…" This time she choked his name off.

A reflection in the framed print on the opposite wall revealed a movement outside, nothing more than a glimmer of motion. Amara ducked as a bullet blasted through the window and embedded itself in the wall next to the print.

She took off like a runner from her mark. With her stomach churning and her fingers stiff, she reached for the bathroom door, yanked it shut. Her action blocked the light, but didn't, probably couldn't, contain anything else.

Knowing she'd be visible as a silhouette, she used the threadbare sleeper sofa for cover. She was both relieved and horrified when a second bullet whizzed past her. Her uncle wasn't the target.

On the other hand, obviously she was.

Casting a fearful look into the darkness, she fought for calm. Options. There had to be at least one other means of escape besides the front door.

She swung her head around. Yes, there! The kitchenette had a window. If she could open it, she could get outside.

Hugging every available dark patch, Amara worked her way over to the window. She pulled and tugged on the latch until the slider stuttered sideways.

A quick look revealed nothing except fog and a swarm of raven tamer vehicles. Two more bullets burst through the front window as she climbed over the sill and hopped down between the cabins.

She wanted to scream, longed to run and hide until the danger and the terror passed. But she maintained her crouch and ordered herself not to make a sound. She only remembered to exhale when everything around her started to spin.

Chills scraped like claws along her spine, over her skin, through her head.

Shut the fear out, she told herself. *Think about McVey.*

She could see the back of his truck from her current position. If she could reach it, she could—what? Not leave. Never leave. Because somewhere in her jumbled head she felt certain she had the answer.

This was about revenge—it had to be—for something she'd done as a child.

She and Yolanda had traded barbs her first night back in the Hollow. So had she and Jake.

Spiders, Amara recalled. Years ago, Yolanda had wanted to terrorize her. For reasons of their own, Jake and Yolanda's brother, Larry, had collected a jarful of the horrible creatures, then put the jar in her bed. Jake in particular had enjoyed the so-called prank.

Had Jake and Yolanda been friends as children? Had Jake and Larry? Amara didn't think so. Why, then, had Jake been so eager to participate in Yolanda's scheme? Because of his younger brother, Jimbo?

From Jake's perspective, it made sense.

But would Jake want Hannah dead? Would he blow up the Red Eye? He certainly could have left the bar without anyone noticing. But why destroy a place he liked?

Unless his plan had been to murder her and cloud her death by killing innocent people with her. Would Jake go that far out of spite? Would anyone?

There had to be more.

The "something" she'd mentioned to McVey tapped

a sly finger on the shoulder of her memory. It almost scratched its way through. But as before, "almost" faded to black, leaving her frustrated and frightened.

Where was McVey? And the paramedics. Surely thirty minutes had passed. Why hadn't they arrived?

Why had she left McVey's backup gun and her cell phone on the table in her uncle's room?

Okay, enough, Amara decided. There was a plus side here. She had McVey's keys in her jacket pocket, and there was a police radio in his truck. She could call the Harden twins for help.

She waited until long wisps of cloud passed across the moon; then she slammed the lid on her terror and ran. She reached the driver's door without incident. Yanking it open, she climbed onto the running board.

And spied a dozen spiders crawling across the seat.

She jerked back as if electrocuted.

Spiders in McVey's truck. Spiders in her uncle's medicine cabinet. Jake would not do this. He'd always been bitter and spiteful, downright hostile toward her, in fact. But torment wasn't his way. He was a hothead, and hotheads tended to want the job done.

The elusive "something" she'd been struggling to identify all day struck her as she backed across the parking lot. Maybe it was the cotton-candy streaks on one of the raven tamers' wagons, but suddenly there it was, front and center in her head. A smear of pink lipstick on the rim of a wineglass in Hannah's kitchen sink. Bright pink. Like the lipstick worn by Willy Sparks and...

"One more step, Amara, and you're a dead woman."

The voice grated along her nerve ends. But Amara halted because she knew. This was no idle threat. Not with three people dead and a bar in smoldering ruins.

Footsteps crunched on the gravel. She saw the gun first,

then the arm, and finally the hatred that spewed like poisoned darts from her cousin Yolanda's glittering blue eyes.

MCVEY STRUGGLED TO RESURFACE. Unfortunately, to push through, he had to battle distorted visions of smoking pots, dripping black blobs and the terror of a young girl as she broke free from the woman holding her. As she ran from the attic at Bellam Manor.

Through the child's eyes, he took in stairwells—long, narrow sets of them—and the jagged bolts of lightning that split the sky above the manor.

The high cliffs beckoned, but he ran from them, over rock and rough ground toward the bridge.

He didn't know why he'd chosen that direction until he looked up and saw a raven flying overhead. It seemed to be leading him. To his death or away from it? Too confused to think, he followed the bird on faith and hoped like hell it would take him someplace far away from the madwoman behind him.

"You must cross Bellam Bridge, Annalee." The raven's voice floated down. Could ravens talk, or had he gone mad, too? "You must cross what she cannot."

The child McVey had been knew the structure had been damaged by a series of recent storms. No one crossed Bellam Bridge these days.

"Run, Annalee," the raven urged. It landed on a damaged support, appeared to gesture with its wings. "You must cross the bridge now!"

McVey glanced back and saw her coming. Sarah, enraged, her arms outstretched, her eyes glowing with madness.

Going now, he decided, plunging onto the bridge.

It pitched and rocked and made dreadful screeching noises that rose above the wild thunder. But it didn't buckle, not even when he tripped and went down hard on his hands and knees.

"Run, Annalee," the raven repeated. "I will not allow her to leave this mountain. Here she has built herself a cage, and here will she remain."

McVey almost lost his footing a second time, but he managed to clutch a thick post and prevent the fall. Too winded to look back, he jumped over a broken plank and landed on all fours on the other side.

Sarah screamed into the howling wind, "It's mine, all of it, by right. Do you hear me? It's mine."

Whatever "it" was, McVey wanted no part of it. But Sarah obviously did.

"You have nothing more to fear," the raven told him calmly. "Be still, and know that she who would see you— who would see all of us—worse than dead will herself never see anything beyond the world she has created in her attic room again."

McVey wasn't quite as certain as the raven appeared to be. He watched until he saw double. Stared unmoving as Sarah stepped onto the bridge.

Stared in shock as, three steps later, she fell through, ranting and cursing, yet somehow able to catch hold of a truss.

Her shrieks joined with the thunder. Together, the sounds wrenched McVey out of his dream.

Amara!

Her name was a thunderbolt in his head. Gaining his feet like a man after a three-day drunk, he brought the motel into focus.

On the ground beside him, R.J. groaned and rolled over. McVey saw blood on his shoulder and hoped the wound wouldn't kill him. Because at the same time he spied R.J., he also spied Lazarus's truck fishtailing toward the old highway.

"Go, McVey." Panting, R.J. rolled onto his elbow. "I can manage. Find whatever bastard did this and put a bullet in him for me."

McVey wiped blood from his cheek, spit it from his mouth. "Not him. Her. Check on your uncle if you can. I'm going for Amara." His features hardened because, damn it, he should have seen this sooner. "And Yolanda."

Chapter Eighteen

Woods and hills shrouded in fog flew by in an eerie blur. Despite her terror—which had peaked when Yolanda and her Luger had stepped from the shadows of a raven tamer wagon—Amara knew where they were headed. Bellam Mountain.

With her hands cuffed behind her and her ankles bound by a rough hemp rope, she could only give her body an angry twist. "What did you do to Uncle Lazarus?" she demanded.

Yolanda snickered. "I slipped a mickey into his milk, of course. Right after R.J. left for a night at Two Toes Joe's bar. Traitor likes it there."

"You call R.J. a traitor?" Amara gave another angry twist.

"I call it as I see it." Her cousin smirked. "Fight all you like, Amara. I stole those handcuffs from Jake. You won't be getting out of them any time soon."

"Yolanda, this is crazy. Why are you—?"

"Shut up," her cousin snapped. She beamed a smile across the cab when Amara wisely broke off. "I love it when I give an order and someone obeys. Especially when that someone is you. Now spill. Did you think it was me, Jake or Larry who put the spiders in Uncle Lazarus's bathroom? Go ahead, you can say. Me, Jake or Larry?"

"Jake."

"Seriously?" She wrinkled her nose. "Why?"

"Revenge. I freaked his brother, Jimbo, out when we were kids. I didn't think you'd go that far, and Larry's got his own quirks and hang-ups to deal with."

"So my brother sleepwalks naked. What does that prove?"

"That he has his own quirks and hang-ups to deal with, and while he might be willing to do you a favor, he's not really a vindictive person. Plus, even though he's a Bellam himself, I always thought Larry was nervous about the whole witch thing. He never possessed any power, but I'm pretty sure he believed we did."

"You think Larry believed, but Jake didn't?"

"Jake's too sexist to believe any female could harm him."

"Bull. What it really boils down to, why you really thought Jake put the spiders in Uncle's bathroom and not me, is because Jake's a guy and I'm not." Yolanda gave the steering wheel a petulant thump. "Why do people think only men can kill with guns? Poison, that's a woman's weapon. Fine, maybe I didn't shoot her, but I got Hannah with the butt end of my Luger. One whack and down she went. Not that it took much muscle on my part. She was pretty hammered by the time I coaxed her over to the main part of the manor."

"You got Hannah to walk all that way on a bad leg?"

"She didn't walk, she limped. Stumbled. Laughed like a loon. But come on, Ammie, we're talking raven tamer whiskey here. A few swigs of that stuff and who even knows you have legs?"

"You got an old woman drunk so you could kill her."

"The old woman was a lush. She dumped three fingers of whiskey into her coffee without a word of encouragement from me. I'll cop to adding more while she was pouring me a glass of that gut-rot raven's blood wine, but honestly? It was superfluous at that point."

Working herself around so she could lean against the door, Amara regarded her cousin's profile. "Call me dense, Yolanda, but I'm still not getting this."

"You're dense." Only Yolanda's eyes slid sideways. "You're also stupid, stupid, stupid." Grinning, she did a little butt dance. "Knowing that makes all the trouble worthwhile."

"*Trouble.* Is that your euphemism for *murder?*" Amara tugged experimentally on her wrists, but, as predicted, the cuffs held. "When did you go insane?"

Her cousin sneered. "You're such a weenie. People die every day. Some do it naturally. Others are helped along. I subscribe to the second way of thinking. And in support of my earlier remark about women and guns, Hannah wasn't the only person I 'helped along.' I also offed the cute jerk with the knife who wanted the bimbo with the overbite instead of me. I admit that night's a bit fuzzy, but I think I put a bullet in her before I did him. Would you believe the bitch pulled a gun on me at exactly the same time I pulled one on her? I mean, talk about your bizarre coincidences."

She didn't know. Yolanda had no idea who she'd murdered in that alley. Growing desperate, Amara worked on freeing her ankles rather than her wrists.

The foggy landscape rushed past as her cousin pounded through ruts and potholes, mindless of the damage she might be inflicting on the truck's undercarriage.

"Yolanda… Ouch. Damn."

"Almost bite your tongue off there, cuz? Not to worry. You'll be dead soon. Won't matter."

"Yeah, I got that part. What I still don't get is why? I know you hate me.…"

"Loathe, despise, put a thousand curses on you that unfortunately never took." Yolanda shrugged. "No point understating things."

"We'll agree we're not friends. I never liked Jake's brother, but I think murdering him would have been a little extreme. So I'm guessing there's a reason other than loathing behind what you've done."

"Well, duh." Yolanda swung the truck with reckless abandon around the remains of a fallen tree. She did her second butt dance to an old Abba song. "Money, money, money. I want it, honey. When the rich man croaks."

Astonishment momentarily blotted out every other emotion. "That's what this is about? Money?"

"Rich man's money. Richest man in the Hollow and the Cove combined's money."

The missing puzzle piece fell into place at last. All the way into place as Amara recalled the contents of their uncle Lazarus's medicine cabinet.

"Oh, my God," she exclaimed softly. "Sunitinib. And everolimus. The first drug was farther back on the shelf. It would have been older."

"Is that doctor talk for 'oh, what a dumb ass I've been'? Which you totally are, and I'd be the last person to argue the point. But bottom line? Uncle Dearest's life is winding down like an eight-day clock ticking through the last few minutes of its final hour."

Amara only half heard her. She'd been blind. She'd seen the drugs the night she'd gone looking for antacid. Seen but hadn't absorbed.

"Saw the trees just fine." She sighed. "Missed the forest completely."

Yolanda ticked a finger. "More doctor talk, I assume, meaning your teeny, tiny mind overlooked what would have been a no-brainer for most first-year med students."

Ignoring her, Amara let her head fall back against the window. "Those drugs are used to treat renal cancer, the newer usually after a failure with the older. But even the new drug didn't have a recent date on it." Her terror momentarily suspended, she regarded her cousin. "Uncle Lazarus has kidney cancer."

"Yes, he does. It's also in his bladder and, fingers crossed, his liver. And how do I know this, you ask, when in all probability he hasn't told a soul?"

"You went through his desk?"

"Nope. One day, R.J. got sick and Uncle had to go to Bangor for a check-up. I offered to drive him. I mean, a girl's gotta suck up, right? We drove, I made a show of leaving the doctor's office, and on a lovely spring day, I stood under an open window in an alley very much like the one where I shot the jerk and the bimbo and I listened to Uncle's doctor tell him he needed tests. Of course, Uncle Lazarus always does what's needed, including getting himself to a lab at some point. The next part was a guess, but a good one, I think."

"He wanted to see the test results," Amara said. "All of them, personally, so he had copies delivered by express mail as soon as they were available."

"Exactly. I retract one 'stupid.' The results arrived. Uncle got uncharacteristically drunk and punched the courier—or you could say messenger—down at Two Toes Joe's bar."

Amara was so far beyond shock, her mind simply went numb. "Did you see the results or just go with your guess?"

"Uncle's drunken punch spoke for itself. It validated my guess well enough."

"So all this death, all these murders, are about money."

"Whacks of money, Amara."

"Did you kill Uncle Lazarus's sister, too?"

"Aunt Maureen? Didn't have to. The old girl smoked herself to death. Thank you very much, Auntie Mo. But I will admit, it was her death that planted the seed in my head. As the seed grew, I said to myself, 'Wait a minute, Yolanda, the old guy must have a will.' So I skulked and I lurked and eventually I said to hell with it. One afternoon, when I knew he and R.J. would be in Bangor, I did what you said and searched Uncle's office. Jackpot."

They clattered over a broken-up section of the road. Amara stole a glance behind them. There were no headlights. Did that mean Yolanda had seen McVey tonight? Seen and… No, not going there, she decided. "Obviously you're named in the will," she said instead.

"Number four on the list," her cousin confirmed. "Good old Uncle thinks I'll be thrilled to inherit the Red Eye. Woo-hoo. You, on the other hand, as number-two heir, were initially in line for Bellam Manor and an offensive amount of cash. I don't remember Hannah's bequest—she was number three—but I do know Aunt Maureen was slated to receive the lion's share of his estate. Here's the best part, though, and the reason I did what I did. According to the terms of Uncle Lazarus's will, if one heir predeceases the others, whatever bequest he or she would have received goes to the next person in line. How cool is that?"

"Too cool." Amara closed her eyes. "So after Aunt Maureen died, I became number one. If I'd died, everything would have gone to Hannah."

"'Would have' being the operative phrase."

"And with Hannah and me both gone, you're the big winner."

"Bigger than big, Amara. Oh, I'll share some of my winnings with my brother, but for the most part Larry's perfectly happy setting off controlled avalanches in the Rockies during the winter and hanging out with his too-

cool-for-school sister—who happens to be a Bellam female and a teeny bit scary when she doesn't get her own
way—in the spring and summer."

"For the record," Amara remarked, "in the bitch-witch
pecking order, you're miles ahead of me."

"Why, thank you, cousin."

"It wasn't a compliment."

"No? Huh. Guess I'll have to make your death doubly
painful. Should anyway." She huffed out a breath. "I'm
pretty sure McVey'll have to go once I do you."

Relief coursed through her. McVey was alive. Thank
God, he was alive. "You're not a witch, Yolanda," she
snapped. "You're a demon from hell."

"Maybe, but I'm a smart one." Her cousin buffed hot
pink fingernails on her jacket. "Wanna know how I way-
laid McVey?"

Amara shot her a look, but Yolanda merely snickered
and sailed on.

"I smucked him with the spare cane Uncle keeps in this
very truck. Had to shoot R.J. first, of course. Not fatally,
mind you, just enough to knock him off his feet. I know,
I know, I should have shot McVey as well, but I've been
trying really hard to think of a way to finish this without
offing him. I mean, it kills me—pun intended—to think
of the waste. The man's smoking hot. Unfortunately, I
can't get around the fact that he's also a freaking great
cop. Too great."

"Meaning you're not an equally great murderer?"

"I'm getting the hang of it—but, no, I'm not a major
league player quite yet."

"Is that your goal, Yolanda? To make the big league?"

"Only in the money column, cousin. Once the killing's
done, it's done. If R.J. can't identify me, he can live. He's
in the will, but lower on the list than me." She widened

her eyes. "I don't need absolutely everything. Just most of it will do."

All Amara could think right then was that Yolanda hadn't killed McVey. She'd knocked him out, but he was alive.

And they were getting very close to Bellam Bridge.

She tried not to notice the baleful looks Yolanda cast her. Fear was an endless slither in her stomach. Her cousin wouldn't be talked out of her plan, and Jake's handcuffs were holding fast.

"I watched you the morning after you got here," Yolanda said at length. "Took some binoculars and Larry's old .30-30 and climbed a tree outside Nana's house. There was a moment when I was tempted to shoot all of you—Uncle Lazarus, McVey and you—when you were together in the kitchen. But it crossed my mind that if I missed, especially if I missed McVey, I'd be screwed. And, well, hey—superhot cop."

"I'll have to remember to thank him for the reprieve."

"You won't be thanking anyone, Amara. My tiny lapse of confidence and lust only gave you a few more days to be scared out of your wits." She waited a beat before asking, "So tell me—because I can't help being curious—was the cute creep with the knife one of Jimmy Sparks's people?"

"No, he was an old enemy of McVey's people."

"I'd say tell McVey he's welcome from me. Unfortunately… yada yada." She jumped on the brake pedal with both feet and almost flung Amara through the windshield.

Grinning, she set the brake. "Road ends here, Ammie." Plucking the Luger from her lap, she straight-armed it so the tip was less than an inch from Amara's forehead. "Now we walk."

Amara forced her lips into a humorless smile. "Or in my case, hop."

Yolanda matched her smile. "If you piss me off, yes. You might actually prefer to hop when you discover where we're going."

"Not Bellam Manor?"

"That would be too cliché, cousin. No, word's out on the sorry state of Bellam Bridge. Why on earth you tried to cross it, no one in either town will ever understand, but you did—or soon will. Tragically, you fell through and died." Eyes gleaming, Yolanda leaned forward to stage-whisper, "Or soon will."

McVey didn't ask Brigham how he'd gotten to the motel or why he'd come. He only knew, if it was the last thing he did, he was going to get Amara back before Yolanda harmed her.

Sweeping a dozen large spiders from McVey's truck, the raven tamer tossed a bulky pack onto the floor and plunked his own bulk in the passenger seat. "Go," he said, and pointed. "That way."

McVey wanted to ignore him, but the big man gripped the steering wheel and matched him stare for stare.

"She's common, McVey. And I know that mountain better than anyone alive."

McVey's curse promised more than pain if Brigham was wrong. He gave it another second, then shoved the truck in gear and spun the wheel—in the opposite direction to the one Yolanda had taken.

Yolanda didn't force her to hop, but after untying Amara's ankles, she knotted the rope to the handcuffs binding her cousin's wrists and wound the other end around her own hand.

"On the very likely chance you decide to make a break

for it," she said, giving the rope a tug that sent pain singing along Amara's arms.

She wouldn't panic, Amara promised herself. Her cousin was clearly crazy. She was also overconfident. And crazy, overconfident people made mistakes.

She hoped.

The wind whipped up as they closed in on the bridge. Not enough to disperse the fog, but enough to stir it around and create patches of white that tended to envelop without warning and vanish the same way.

"I wouldn't waste my energy screaming," Yolanda advised. "I whacked McVey plenty hard with Uncle's cane."

Amara watched for the bridge. "Are you trying to convince me or yourself, Yolanda?"

"Got my gun. Got you. If McVey shows, I'll get him, too. That'll leave Jake in charge until Ty gets back from his honeymoon, and by then… Evidence? What evidence? I might have to lower myself and convince Jake that I've really been hot for him all these years—eww—but needs must in a situation like this, don't you agree?"

"I wouldn't know, having never been in a situation like this."

"Bitch." Yolanda gave the rope a vicious jerk. "Ah, excellent. Bellam Bridge." She reeled Amara in as she might a fish on a line. "What a wreck."

Amara jerked away from the finger Yolanda stroked between her shoulder blades.

"I'm betting you won't make ten steps without falling through." Her cousin looked up. "Oh, nuts, the moon's gone out. But no worries, I have a flashlight. Couldn't risk missing the grand finale, could I? Although technically, McVey will be the finale—still pissed about that one—and R.J. if necessary."

Unable to wrest her eyes from the bridge, Amara asked,

"Were you born with no conscience, or did it die the day you killed Hannah?"

"I killed Hannah at night." Yolanda poked Amara's shoulder. "Walk."

"You want me to die in handcuffs? Won't that look suspicious, even to someone with Jake's limited policing skills?"

"I am so going to enjoy watching you fall," her cousin snarled. "It'll be Christmas in May." Visibly annoyed now, she used her left hand to shove the gun into Amara's back while her right pulled out and inserted a small key in the lock.

The handcuffs fell away. The gun dug deeper.

"Have a nice trip, Ammie."

Her push sent Amara to her knees on the rocky roadbed.

Without making a sound, a raven swished out of the fog. Its talons grazed the top of Yolanda's head. When her cousin swore and waved her arms, Amara took advantage and rolled quickly sideways.

The raven swooped again, but this time Yolanda struck its body with her gun. The bird gave a raucous caw, spread its wings—and began to spark. It fell, beak open and smoking, to the ground.

Furious, Yolanda whipped her gun around while she scoured the trees. Amara sucked in a bolstering breath. *Go big or go home,* she reflected and, using her shoulder, went for her cousin's knees.

If the bridge had been susceptible to sound vibrations, Yolanda's shriek would have brought it down. She fell sideways but kicked out hard and caught Amara in the hip with the heel of her boot.

Wind swirled a thick patch of fog between them. Unfortunately that left only one direction for Amara to take. If she wanted to escape, she'd have to cross Bellam Bridge.

She knew there must be a raven tamer in the vicinity. There often was, and they hadn't all gone down to the Hollow for the parade. If this one was smart, however, he or she would stay out of sight.

Behind her, Yolanda fired several bullets.

"Where are you?" she demanded. Her voice echoed into and back out of the chasm below. She fired again and again. "I've got tons of ammo, cousin. Come out where I can see you or I'll keep shooting into the fog."

Amara crouched behind one of the damaged supports. Her heart had long ago made a home for itself in her throat. Should she attempt to cross the bridge or go wide and circle?

She dipped as a bullet zinged off the support and whizzed past her ear. The near hit made the choice for her. She'd go with the bridge, where the fog was thickest and Yolanda might not think to look.

Uttering every prayer she knew, Amara started across on trembling hands and knees.

A hoarse caw tore through the damp air. Glancing up, she thought she saw a raven go into a nosedive. Several yards back, Yolanda screamed.

Grateful for the distraction, Amara crawled on.

The planks sagged and made dreadful noises, but thankfully none of them broke all the way through.

Her teeth were chattering, she realized. She had splinters in her palms and at least one nail had spiked her knee.

More caws reached her and too many shrieks to count. Then suddenly she heard a thud, like boot heels on wood.

Her eyes closed and her heart plunged into her stomach. Yolanda was on the bridge.

She needed to move faster. No time now to test her weight on the planks.

Squinting through a gap in the fog, she spied a support

post. A raven sat unmoving on one of the pegs that jutted out of it. Unlike its predecessors, however, this bird didn't dive. It simply sat and stared.

A watcher, she thought, and recalled Brigham's words about emissary ravens. Breathing carefully, she offered a heartfelt "I hope you're watching for someone good."

"Its talons are caught in my hair!" Yolanda screeched. "Where are these stupid birds coming from? They're in my freaking hair!"

She was close, Amara realized. Fear spiked—then shot off the scale as Yolanda's frantic fingers trapped her ankle.

But only for a moment. Amara was tugging on her foot when one of the planks gave a long, low groan—and snapped.

Yolanda warbled out a sound between a scream and a sob and fought to grab the broken wood. One moment her fingers were clawing at the splintered end; the next they were gone and only slithering coils of fog remained.

Amara stared at the empty space for several shocked seconds, unable to move or to think. Stared until the raven watching her released a startled caw.

Her head shot up. The wood beneath her protested. It didn't snap as it had for Yolanda. Instead it pulled away from the side of the bridge.

Her scrabbling fingers found a rusted metal bar. But the bar was pulling away as well, and it was too narrow for her to hold in any case.

Overhead, the raven cawed again. And again and again. When it stopped, a strong hand grasped her wrist.

"I've got you, Red." McVey's voice reached her from the girder above. "Just hold on tight and don't look down."

A dozen emotions swamped her, but the one that stood out, that caused her breath to hitch, was that Yolanda hadn't lied. McVey was alive!

Half a lifetime passed in Amara's tortured mind before her knees touched solid wood again. Although solid was a questionable description for the worn plank that currently held not only her weight but also McVey's. Risking it, she threw her arms around his neck and crushed her mouth to his.

"You came," she said between kisses. "How did you know where to come?"

Taking her face in his hands, he looked into her eyes. "Once I figured out who the killer had to be, only the manor made sense. We took a roundabout route."

"We?"

"Brigham's here."

A sigh rushed out. "He brought his ravens, didn't— Oh, my God, Yolanda!"

She pivoted, heard the plank beneath them groan.

Catching her arms, McVey stilled her. "Don't bounce too much, Red. Even raven tamer ingenuity has its limits where ancient bridges are concerned."

"So we lead you to believe." Brigham's growl came from a cloud of fog. "Yolanda's right here. The rope she was holding tangled on one of the supports. I've got her now. Do you want me to haul the murdering witch up or develop butterfingers and end the problem tonight?"

McVey raised a brow. "Your call, Amara."

Now that the worst of her terror had subsided, Amara could hear Yolanda's combination of girlish squeals and vicious threats. "Well, damn." Sighing, she glanced up at him. "You know, I'd love to be lofty about this and prove how much better I am than her, but I guess I'm only human in the end. Haul her up, Brigham," she said. "She's insane, and one day I might actually pity her for that. But for now? I want the witch to burn."

Chapter Nineteen

The way McVey saw it, where there was crime there should be punishment. It didn't always work that way, but when it did, there wasn't a whole lot that made him feel better. Unless you switched gears and started talking sex. Specifically, sex with Amara, which he hoped would cap off one of the most gut-wrenching, yet strangely satisfying nights of his life.

Five long hours after he'd pulled her up onto Bellam Bridge, Amara pulled him to a stop on the main street of the Hollow. "How on earth can you call anything about this night satisfying, McVey? Uncle Lazarus is in a hospital in Bangor...."

"Resting comfortably, Red." He held up two fingers at the raven tamer who was manning the street-side bar, which, in strict legal terms, didn't exist. "You talked to his doctor. Your uncle's day-to-day. Has been for quite some time."

"A fact you apparently knew and I didn't."

"He told me the morning after I arrested him for punching the courier. He asked me not to tell anyone. You're part of anyone."

"I'm his niece, McVey. I'm also a physician. I could have..."

"What? Said, 'There, there,' and prescribed morphine

for the pain? He didn't want that. Private and proud's the way he's built."

She blew out a breath. "Damn…him for keeping a secret like that and you for being right. Damn Yolanda, too, for being…well, Yolanda, and wanting everything for herself."

Accepting two glasses of raven's blood from the grinning tamer, McVey handed her one. "You know her lawyer's going to plead insanity."

"He doesn't have to claim what's perfectly obvious." She watched animated ravens swoop and soar around a still-lively Main Street. "I'm not sure I think she was completely sane as a kid. And I've always thought her brother, Larry, was borderline."

"A man who handles explosives is only borderline sane?" Draping an arm across her shoulders, McVey summoned a lazy smile. "That idea might shake some people's faith a bit. Fortunately, any faith I ever had was shaken apart when I worked in Homicide. There are no absolutes, Amara. In the end, all anyone can do is his or her best."

"Thank you, Mike Brady. But back in this world, I still have questions."

"Will there be sex after they're answered?"

She laughed, and the sound of it made him want to drag her off the street and into the station house.

"Looks like I was right way back when, Chief McVey. You have definite animal—specifically wolf—instincts and appetites." She ran teasing fingers through the ends of his hair. "In this life anyway."

His eyes narrowed. "I knew we'd get here at some point. You're going to remind me I have Bellam blood in my background, aren't you?"

"You know you do. I don't have to remind you. When Nola Bellam married Hezekiah Blume, she already had a child, a daughter. According to one version of the Bellam legend—not to mention your recurring nightmare—it was Nola's daughter, Annalee, who brought about Sarah's confinement in the attic at Bellam Manor. In your dream, Sarah fell through a broken plank, but like Yolanda, she didn't plunge into the chasm below."

"Was Annalee a witch?"

"No one knows. With a little feathered help, though, she took mad Sarah out of the local picture." Amara angled her head. "Kind of the way you did with Yolanda tonight. Spooky, isn't it?"

"Very. But it was me and Brigham, not me alone on the bridge."

"I'd speculate that Annalee has more than one descendant, McVey. And every raven tamer has two parents."

"Pretty sure Brigham won't appreciate that particular speculation."

"He should. The mix of bloodlines is probably why he's so adept—one, at taming live ravens and, two, at creating animated ones. Which brings me to my really big question."

"How did we find you?"

"I already know that. You had to figure Yolanda would want to kill me in or around Bellam Manor, and what better way to do it than by using the bridge as her murder weapon? No, my big question is why did the bridge suddenly become crossable after Yolanda and I both fell through?"

"You and Yolanda didn't know where to walk. Brigham did. The raven tamers dislike intrusions into their privacy. They rigged the bridge to work safely for them and only them. For the rest of us, each crossing was a roll of the dice."

"Why does that sound illegal?"

"Call it marginally unethical, and think of it this way.

The land on both sides of that bridge belongs to your uncle Lazarus. He's the only person legally entitled to file a lawsuit against them."

"Which he won't do because he's enjoying the fact that the person who killed Hannah was caught by one."

"The person who killed Hannah and tried on more than one occasion to kill you." McVey tapped his wineglass to hers. "She might have been in your uncle's will, but Yolanda was never your uncle's favorite niece. He mentioned something tonight about liking her mother and cutting Yolanda a break strictly for that reason."

"Yolanda's mother died in a car accident while I was in med school." Amara paused to watch a meticulously choreographed flock of ravens wing through the sky overhead. "Brigham's distraction helped. One of his animated ravens got its talons stuck in Yolanda's hair. She panicked. If I hadn't been so terrified, I'd have enjoyed watching her freak. She's lucky Brigham was there to pull her up."

"She's lucky that rope she had wrapped around her wrist caught on one of the supports."

Amara smiled. "I'm not thinking she'll see it that way." She paused then said, "It was the pink lipstick that gave it to me. Pink lipstick on a wineglass in Hannah's kitchen sink. Suddenly, I realized. We went through Hannah's things. She didn't wear makeup."

"And Willy Sparks had no reason to want Hannah dead."

"So Yolanda it was. Had to be. What about you? What gave it to you?"

"Her brother works with explosives. She'd have known how to set charges, and anyone can make a Molotov cocktail."

Amara frowned. "Do we know why she blew up the bar? Other than trying to kill me, of course, which would have been her primary motive. But I mean, destroy her own workplace?"

McVey shrugged. "I imagine she was making a statement of some sort."

"I suppose it makes sense from Yolanda's point of view. Uncle Lazarus left the Red Eye to her in his will. She was…unimpressed to say the least."

"I also saw the pink lipstick a split second before she whacked me with your uncle's cane," McVey said. "Then everything went from pink to black."

Tipping her head to the side, Amara rested it on his shoulder. "You have to admit, it's been a hugely eventful day."

"More than you probably know. I got word from Lieutenant Michaels's captain. Jimmy Sparks is dying."

"There seems to be a lot of that going around."

"His position within the family has been taken over by his sister. Rumor has it she's much less vindictive than her brother."

"I really, seriously, hope that's true." When a raven glided in for a landing on one of the wagons, Amara waved her glass at it. "That bird's been popping up everywhere I go since we got back to town. I recognize it by the small gray streak on its head."

McVey grinned. "At the risk of repeating myself, male ravens around here have damn good taste."

She traced the outline of its sleek black wings and shiny feathered head. "I wonder if he's the same raven I saw on the bridge."

"You saw a raven on the bridge?"

She batted his stomach. "Yes, I did, and so did you. You must have. It was sitting right above your head."

"Are you sure it was real?"

"Positive. The tamers are good, but no one's that good.

That raven, like this one, was staring at me. Turning back to the legend, it's possible he was staring on behalf of someone who sent him."

"And that would be?"

"Not Yolanda's brother. And not Jake. I'd say Uncle Lazarus, except he doesn't believe."

"That you know of."

Amara chuckled. "My uncle's a practical man, McVey. Practical men don't buy into legends."

"Once again—that you know of."

"Right." Laughing, she turned to face him and hook an arm around his neck. "So, ignoring the raven, which isn't as easy as you might think, where does that leave us?"

He slid his fingers through her hair, nudged her head up a notch. "I guess the answer to that depends on you. You're going to be a very rich woman in a very short time. You'll be able to come and go as you please. Or stay if you'd prefer."

She regarded him through her lashes. "While I'm torn, I have to admit I'm leaning."

The raven gave an irritated caw and, even to McVey's eyes, appeared to glare at them.

Glancing over, Amara frowned. "Okay, now I'm the one who's spooked. That raven looks scarily like Uncle Lazarus in disapproval mode. Which makes me think I'm starting to buy in to the local legends, and I mean all the way in, because, if you think about it, what did Sarah Bellam ultimately want?"

"Hezekiah's fortune," McVey said without hesitation.

"Exactly. And her solution to the problem of attaining it, once she discovered she was pregnant with Ezekiel's child, was to eliminate anyone and everyone who might also lay claim to it. Add in the fact that she was a vindictive witch whose lover wanted her sister more than he wanted her, and you have the perfect recipe for murder. Two Blumes and a Bellam in Sarah's case."

"If she'd succeeded, and allowing for the fact that Lazarus's sister died without anyone's help, Yolanda had an eerily similar plan." McVey ran a thumb across her lower lip. "Kill you—a Bellam. Hannah—a Blume. And wait for Lazarus—also a Blume—to succumb."

"Two Blumes and a Bellam," Amara said. "And you thwarted their plans in both lifetimes. That's an impressive score, Annalee."

A smile touched McVey's mouth as the raven flapped impatient wings. "No comment."

Amara finished her wine. "A little bird—not him—told me Ty and Molly have decided to relocate to Florida. He also mentioned that late this very afternoon you were offered Ty's job here in the Hollow. One chief, two towns and the saddest excuse for a medical clinic I've ever seen… Am I avoiding the real question here?"

"If the question is where should we have sex, I'll be happy to supply the answer."

She teased him with her eyes. "Answer this instead. Do you want me to stay?"

He held her gaze. "Yes."

"Then I'll stay."

"Good answer, Red."

As he lowered his head, McVey saw the raven spread its wings. It stared a moment longer, then flew off as silently as it had arrived.

If there was anything at all to the local legends, he hoped Lazarus Blume would fall asleep smiling tonight.

* * * * *

REQUEST YOUR FREE BOOKS!
2 FREE NOVELS PLUS 2 FREE GIFTS!

HARLEQUIN
INTRIGUE

BREATHTAKING ROMANTIC SUSPENSE

YES! Please send me 2 FREE Harlequin Intrigue® novels and my 2 FREE gifts (gifts are worth about $10). After receiving them, if I don't wish to receive any more books, I can return the shipping statement marked "cancel." If I don't cancel, I will receive 6 brand-new novels every month and be billed just $4.74 per book in the U.S. or $5.24 per book in Canada. That's a savings of at least 14% off the cover price! It's quite a bargain! Shipping and handling is just 50¢ per book in the U.S. and 75¢ per book in Canada.* I understand that accepting the 2 free books and gifts places me under no obligation to buy anything. I can always return a shipment and cancel at any time. Even if I never buy another book, the two free books and gifts are mine to keep forever.

182/382 HDN F42N

Name	(PLEASE PRINT)	
Address		Apt. #
City	State/Prov.	Zip/Postal Code

Signature (if under 18, a parent or guardian must sign)

Mail to the **Harlequin® Reader Service:**
IN U.S.A.: P.O. Box 1867, Buffalo, NY 14240-1867
IN CANADA: P.O. Box 609, Fort Erie, Ontario L2A 5X3

Are you a subscriber to Harlequin Intrigue books
and want to receive the larger-print edition?
Call 1-800-873-8635 or visit www.ReaderService.com.

* Terms and prices subject to change without notice. Prices do not include applicable taxes. Sales tax applicable in N.Y. Canadian residents will be charged applicable taxes. Offer not valid in Quebec. This offer is limited to one order per household. Not valid for current subscribers to Harlequin Intrigue books. All orders subject to credit approval. Credit or debit balances in a customer's account(s) may be offset by any other outstanding balance owed by or to the customer. Please allow 4 to 6 weeks for delivery. Offer available while quantities last.

Your Privacy—The Harlequin® Reader Service is committed to protecting your privacy. Our Privacy Policy is available online at www.ReaderService.com or upon request from the Harlequin Reader Service.

We make a portion of our mailing list available to reputable third parties that offer products we believe may interest you. If you prefer that we not exchange your name with third parties, or if you wish to clarify or modify your communication preferences, please visit us at www.ReaderService.com/consumerchoice or write to us at Harlequin Reader Service Preference Service, P.O. Box 9062, Buffalo, NY 14269. Include your complete name and address.

HI13R

"Maybe you don't understand the fine line between snooping and jail. Breaking and entering is—"

"I'm going with you." Donning a hat and gloves, Gillian turned to look at him.

Austin was smiling at her as if amused.

"What?" she said, suddenly feeling uncomfortable under his scrutiny. She knew it was silly. He'd seen her at her absolute worst.

"You just look so…cute," he said. "Clearly, breaking the law excites you."

She smiled in spite of herself. It had been a while since a man had complimented her. But it wasn't breaking the law that excited her.

She breathed in the freezing air. It stung her lungs, but made her feel more alive than she had in years. Fear drove her steps along with hope.

At the dark alley, Austin slowed. It was late enough that there were lights on in the houses.

"Come on," Austin said, and they started to turn down the alley.

A vehicle came around the corner, moving slowly. Gillian felt the headlights wash over them, and she let out a worried sound as she froze in midstep.

Her moment of panic didn't subside when she saw that it was a sheriff's department vehicle.

"Austin?" she whispered, not sure what to do.

He turned to her and pulled her into his arms. Her mouth opened in surprise, and the next thing she knew, he was kissing her. At first, she was too stunned to react. But after a moment, she put her arms around his neck and lost herself in the kiss.

As the headlights of the sheriff's car washed over them, she let out a small helpless moan as Austin deepened the kiss, drawing her even closer.

The sheriff's car went on past, and she felt a pang of regret. Slowly, Austin drew back a little. His gaze locked with hers, and for a moment they stood like that, their quickened warm breaths coming out in white clouds.

"Sorry."

She shook her head. She wasn't sorry. She felt…light-headed, happy, as if helium-filled. She thought she might drift off into the night if he let go of her.

"Are you okay?" he asked, looking worried.

She touched the tip of her tongue to her lower lip. "Great. Never better."

Find out what happens next in
DELIVERANCE AT CARDWELL RANCH
by New York Times *bestselling author B.J. Daniels,*
available December 2014,
only from Harlequin Intrigue.

HARLEQUIN®

INTRIGUE®